PENGUIN ARCHIVE

The Maverick Pig

Wang Xiaobo

1952–1997

A PENGUIN SINCE 2023

Wang Xiaobo

The Maverick Pig

Translated by Yan Yan and Eric Abrahamsen

PENGUIN ARCHIVE

PENGUIN BOOKS

UK | USA | Canada | Ireland | Australia
India | New Zealand | South Africa

Penguin Books is part of the Penguin Random House group of companies
whose addresses can be found at global.penguinrandomhouse.com.

Penguin Random House UK,
One Embassy Gardens, 8 Viaduct Gardens, London SW11 7BW

penguin.co.uk

Penguin
Random House
UK

The Pleasure of Thinking first published in the United States of America by
Astra House 2023
First published in Penguin Classics 2023
This selection published in Penguin Classics 2025
001

Set in 11.2/13.75pt Dante MT Std
Typeset by Jouve (UK), Milton Keynes
Printed and bound in Great Britain by Clays Ltd, Elcograf S.p.A.

The authorized representative in the EEA is Penguin Random House Ireland, Morrison
Chambers, 32 Nassau Street, Dublin D02 YH68

A CIP catalogue record for this book is available from the British Library

ISBN: 978-0-241-74731-5

Penguin Random House is committed to a sustainable future
for our business, our readers and our planet. This book is made from
Forest Stewardship Council® certified paper.

Contents

The Silent Majority

I

In *The Tin Drum*, Günter Grass wrote of a boy who didn't want to grow up. Young Oskar finds the world around him too absurd, and quietly resolves to always remain a child. Whereupon some otherworldly power fulfills his wish and he becomes a midget. This story is a little on the fantastical side, but very illuminating. Though it's impossible to always remain a child, it is possible to always remain silent. Many people around him have personalities much like mine – on public occasions we won't say a word, but we can hardly stop talking in private. Put another way, we will say anything to people we trust, and nothing to those we can't. At first I thought this was because we had lived through the cruelties of the Cultural Revolution, but later I discovered this is common among all Chinese people. The writer Lung Yingtai,* exasperated, once asked why Chinese people never spoke. She had lived abroad for many years, and

---

* Lung Yingtai is a very respected Taiwanese essayist and cultural critic who also served as Taiwan's first cultural bureau chief (1999–2003) and first minister of culture (2012–2014).

had more or less become a foreigner, frank and plainspoken. She viewed silence as a form of cowardice, but this is incorrect; silence is a lifestyle, one chosen not only by Chinese, but also by foreigners.

Here's one example I know of: Dmitri Shostakovich, a composer from the former Soviet Union. There was a long period of time during which he only wrote music, refusing to say a word. Later, he dictated a thick book of memoirs, signed his name on each page, and then died. As I understand it, the subject of his memoirs is for the most part his experience of keeping silent. I found great pleasure in reading the book – of course, I myself was in silence at the time. But I lent the book to a friend of mine who belonged to the circles of speech, and he gained no pleasure from it whatsoever. He found it dismal and depressing. One passage in the book described the Soviet Union in the 1930s, when people were abruptly disappearing, everyone was very frightened and no one spoke to one another. When neighbors had a dispute they didn't dare quarrel, and so expressed themselves by other means, which was to spit into each other's tea-kettles. I haven't a clue as to what Shostakovich looked like, but every time I imagine him doing this I burst out laughing. My friend did not laugh at all when he read this passage; he felt that spitting was ugly, low-class, and unenlightened. I hardly dared debate the point with him – further debate would have fallen under the purview of speech, and speech is the line of demarcation between the world of yin and yang.

Readers of *The Tin Drum* know that young Oskar

changes his mind later, and grows up. I have chosen to speak now, meaning that I am no longer young Oskar, I am old Oskar. Now I agree, of course, that spitting in other people's teakettles is low-class and unenlightened, but certain similar things continue to happen around me. Here's an example familiar to any apartment dweller: if someone keeps leaving their bicycle outside your door, blocking your way, you don't have to keep silent. You can call the neighborhood residential committee, or talk to the bicycle owner directly: 'Comrade, please recall the Five Lectures and Four Beauties.'* As for the language he may use in return, I can make no guarantees. At the very least I expect he'll call you 'nosy,' and if you happen to be a woman he might call you a 'nosy biddy,' regardless of whether you're old enough to be a grandmother or not. Of course you can always choose the way of silence in expressing your displeasure, and let the air out of his tires. Just take care that he doesn't see you doing it. Or you can do something worse, which I won't recommend: stick a tack in his tire. Some people pull the tack out again afterward, making it very difficult for the bicycle owner to find and fix the leak. If the bicycle can be moved, then taking it someplace where the owner is

---

* 'The Five Lectures, Four Beauties, and Three Loves' are ideological education slogans promoted in China in the early 1980s. The Five Lectures refer to civilization, politeness, hygiene, order, and morality. The Four Beauties refer to mind, language, behavior, and environment. The Three Loves refer to love for the People's Republic of China, for socialism, and for the Communist Party of China.

unlikely to find it is also an option. I'll stop here, before I give anyone ideas. All this puts me in mind of what Foucault said, that discourse is power. That ought to be switched around: power means discourse. In terms of the above examples, if you're going to say 'Five Lectures and Four Beauties' to someone, you'd better be wearing a red armband.* In my understanding even a red armband might not be enough: a police uniform would be better. Saying 'Five Lectures and Four Beauties' is a positive thing, naturally, but it's still safest to back it up with force or status. And now you see why, when my friend started talking about Shostakovich, and ugliness and enlightenment, I kept silent. He was a very good friend, but I was still afraid he might give me up.

Most people enter the classroom by the age of seven. I believe it was a little earlier for me, because as far back as I can remember there was a loudspeaker installed outside which kept up a racket throughout the daylight hours. From this speech I learned that one could smelt steel in an open earthen hearth. These resembled the ranges we used for cooking but with a small bellows attached, which would buzz and hum like a group of dung beetles in flight. They smelted cherry red flakes of metal, stuck together in blobs that looked like cow manure. That was steel, an uncle holding a drill rod told me. I was six, and for a long time afterward whenever I heard the word *steel*, I'd think of cow manure. From

* A red armband is worn by the local citizens who are part of the neighborhood residential committee.

that speech I also learned that one mu[*] of land can produce three hundred jin[†] of grain; then we nearly starved
to death. In short, ever since I was young I haven't had
much faith in the spoken world, and the more vehement
the voice, the more fervently it is pitched, the more I
doubt. This habit of doubt had its origins in my starv-
ing belly. Compared with any speech, starvation holds
the greater truth. I had another bad habit, in addition to
doubting speech, and that was eating pencils. In elem-
entary school, I'd start eating a pencil the moment I was
seated at my desk. They were the kind of pencils with
an eraser on the butt, one mao three fen each.[‡] I'd start
at the back and eat the soft delicious eraser first, then
the pliable metal band. Past that, the wooden shaft was
tasteless and unappealing, but it had a perfumed sort of
scent that drove me to keep eating. Finally, there would
be nothing left but the core of lead, which I'd wrap in a
rubber band and continue to use. It wasn't just pencils:
my textbooks, exercise books and even desktops were
edible. Some I consumed altogether; others I left gnawed
beyond recognition. There is a truth here, too, though
one that has not been expressed in words: starvation can
turn a child into a termite.

---

* Mu is a Chinese unit of land measurement which can vary
with location, usually describing 666 square meters.

† Jin is a Chinese unit of weight measurement corresponding
to 500 grams.

‡ The Chinese yuan is divided into mao and fen: ten mao are
needed for one yuan, and ten fen for one mao.

There is a great misconception in the world, which is that speech conveys people's ideas. If that were the case, then speech would be the perfect embodiment of thought. I say it's a misconception because there is always a hidden meaning to things, and speech can convey much which seems contradictory to what is said. Ever since I began to be aware of things I've heard people say: *Our generation was born in a sacred time; how blessed we are; to us is given the sacred mission of liberating all the world's suffering people*, and so forth. People of a certain age found this talk deeply inspiring, they loved to hear it. But I was always a little doubtful: how did I manage to stumble into so many wonderful things? Furthermore, I found this way of talking too unreserved. And reservation was a part of my upbringing. One day during the three years of trouble,* our family sat down to dinner and found a little piece of bacon in every bowl. When my younger brother saw this, he was unable to contain his elation, he ran to our balcony and shouted for all the world to hear: our family has meat for dinner! Then he was dragged back inside by my father and beaten savagely. This sort of education has left me rather withdrawn. So, listening to others talk about how blessed we are, how sacred our mission, how others are suffering but we do not suffer, I always think: supposing we really are as lucky as all that, wouldn't it be better to keep it to ourselves? Of course, I'm not saying I won't carry

---

* This refers to the Great Leap Forward (1958 to 1962), where in the last three years, millions of people starved to death.

out my sacred duty. But here's what I think about all the world's suffering people: instead of constantly telling them how we're going to liberate them and punish their oppressors, wouldn't it be better to keep quiet, and then one day liberate them all of a sudden, and give them an unexpected treat? In short, I'm always considering the practical aspect of things, and considering them very carefully. Childhood experience, upbringing, and cautious nature have all led me to keep silent.

2

When I was young, speech seemed to me like a cold pool of water, it always gave me goose bumps. But no matter what, people come into this world as to the water's edge, and they've got to jump in sooner or later. I never imagined I would keep silent right up to the age of forty; if I had, I might not have had the courage to go on living. But at any rate, the speech I heard was not always that crazy – it was crazy and sane by turns. Before the age of fourteen, I hadn't yet resolved to live a life of silence.

When we were young, it was our place to listen to the speech of others. Later, when people of my age began themselves to speak, it made a terrible impression on me. A friend of mine wrote a book about her misfortunes during the Cultural Revolution, the book was titled *Blood Lineage*. As you can probably guess, her family background was considered problematic. She wanted me to write a preface to the book, which got me thinking about the things I had seen and heard during those years. When the Cultural Revolution began I was fourteen years old, in the first year of middle school. One day one part of our class suddenly belonged to the 'Five Reds,' while another part belonged to the 'Five Blacks.' My own situation was an exception; it wasn't clear to which group I belonged. Of course, this red and black business wasn't our own invention, and we hadn't initiated the change. In that sense we were not to blame. A few among us should be held responsible for bullying classmates, is all.

As I see it, the red students had all at once gained a great advantage, and thus deserved congratulation. Our black classmates were all at once saddled with great misfortune, and deserved sympathy. But before I could go around expressing my congratulations or sympathy, some red students shaved their heads, strapped on big leather belts, and stood at the gate of the school asking everyone who entered: What's your background? They questioned their own classmates particularly closely, and when they heard tell of a background they did not approve of, they would hiss one word between clenched teeth: *Whelp*! Of course I could understand their delight at suddenly belonging to the Five Reds, but that they should therefore call their classmates whelps in public was surely going too far. I thought then what I think now: speech may have a great deal to teach us, but good and evil are nevertheless self-evident. What speech is forever teaching us is that we are born unequal. That some should be high and some low is an eternal truth, though you may choose to disregard it.

When I was in sixth grade, the reading given over the summer was *A Letter from the South*. It was about the Vietnamese people's struggle to resist the United States and save their country, and it was full of executions, beatings, and torture. Reading it filled me with the strangest ideas. I was entering puberty then, more or less on the verge of sexual deviance. What I'm saying is this: suppose that education had had its full intended effect; suppose those 'tenders of the human garden,' those 'engineers of the human soul,' had realized their designs for me; how could I possibly have escaped with my humanity, and resisted becoming bloodthirsty and cruel? Fortunately, people do not learn only from books, they also learn from silence, and this is the chief reason for the survival of my humanity. As for speech, what it taught me was: all 'bull-demons' and 'snake-spirits' must be swept aside, the Cultural Revolution must be carried out to the bitter end. During that time, speech stood in direct opposition to humanity. To believe it entirely would be to relinquish one's humanity.

3

I'll explain how my humanity survived intact: At the very beginning of the Cultural Revolution, I was living on a university campus. One day, returning from outside the campus, I met a large crowd entering by the front gate, their voices pitched high; of course they debated in the popular argot of the day, and in addition to Chairman Mao's teachings, they kept bringing up the 'Six Points.'

These were rules that the central government had issued regarding the progression of the Cultural Revolution, one of which was 'Conduct Verbal Struggle, Not Armed Struggle': a rule simply made to be broken. One person stood at the center of this quarrelling group, but his lips were tightly sealed, he didn't say a word, and there appeared to be blood at the corner of his mouth. Half the students present were pressing him with questions and urging him to speak, the other half were protecting him, telling him to keep silent. This was unusual. As for the rest of the trailing crowd, they were mostly boys of about my age, their lips tightly closed, not saying a word, no blood on their mouths, following behind like damned souls. Some of the college students wanted to hold them back but couldn't – when they blocked the way forward the boys just went around them, keeping silent throughout. This was a strange sight indeed, because the boys from our compound were typically ferocious. They thought nothing of quarreling or fighting, and even college students might not have been a match for them, but today they were surprisingly docile. I immediately joined them and asked what was happening but, strangely, the boys ignored me. Their mouths tightly closed and their eyes straight ahead, they marched forward steadfastly – as if they were all in the grip of some mass hysteria.

As we understand mass hysteria, there's one type where the subjects do not speak, only flail and dance about. Another type results in unceasing chatter, without the flailing. All that the two types have in common is a complete disconnect between that which is thought and that which is expressed. In the northern village in Yunnan where I was a sent-down youth, there was mass hysteria among some of the women, one of whom – if you were inclined to believe her – was the spirit of a fox that had died many years ago. She constantly argued and fought with her husband (who – again if you accepted the premise – was a beast), and demanding that, as a fox, she should be fed meat. When presented with a chunk of flesh, however, she demanded that it be cooked and served with garlic. Obviously, this was ill-suited to a fox's diet, and in fact it was she, not it, that wanted to eat meat. The Cultural Revolution, on the other hand, did seem a bit like mass hysteria, in that what people were thinking was not what they were shouting out loud. Of course, this interpretation takes into account the world of the yin. If you only consider the world of the yang, the conclusion must be that all that violence and chaos really was to protect Chairman Mao, and to protect the Party core.

But the boys from the college campus were not hysterical. I grabbed one I knew well and got the whole story out of him: Two students had met that morning, and started arguing about their differing points of view. The argument went on, and eventually turned into a fight. One of them was hurt, and sent to hospital. The other wasn't hurt, and so was naturally blamed as the aggressor; this was the boy now walking at the head of the group. In theory, the crowd was on its way to some organization or other (either the Campus Revolution Committee or the Preparations Committee, I can't remember which) to state their case but in truth they

were just engaged in aimless Brownian motion* around
the campus. There was another piece to the story: The
wounded student had been beaten shapeless, and a part
of his ear could not be located. Some Agatha Christie-
style reasoning determined that the piece of ear could
only be in the mouth of the student who had adminis-
tered the beating, providing he hadn't swallowed it. This
particular gentleman not only had a violent temper, but
could bite repeatedly. Anyway, he now had two choices:
either spit the ear out in front of everyone, proving his
dastardliness, or swallow it. When I heard all of this I
instantly joined the following crowd, pressing my lips
together, clamping my jaw shut, even feeling I held
something slightly salty in my mouth.

Now I must admit I didn't see the conclusion of this
business; the day was getting on, and there would have
been trouble if I'd returned home late. But I was very
wrapped up in the outcome of events; I hardly slept that
night. Someone else told me how it ended: the biter
finally spat out the ear, and was then apprehended. I
don't know what you'll make of this story, but at the time
I felt as if I'd been relieved of a great weight: humanity
had ultimately prevailed. Humans will not eat their own
kind, nor swallow a piece of another human. I bring this
story up to illustrate a little of what I've learned from

---

* Brownian motion is the random movement of a particle
as a result of collision with surrounding liquids or gaseous
molecules. It is named after the botanist Robert Brown, who
discovered the phenomenon in 1827.

silence. You may say that all these things are not enough, but they are good things – though my methods of study were unorthodox.

By proposing a college student who bites people as a model of humanity, I will certainly anger some. But I have my reasons. A violent-tempered person given to using his teeth is yet unwilling to swallow the flesh of others: there's something particularly powerful about this lesson. Besides, during the course of the Cultural Revolution we scarcely had any better models to learn from.

For a time you would often hear older people saying our generation was no good; among us were the Red Guards of the Cultural Revolution who were of low character. Considering that we weren't products of orphanages but brought up properly in schools, our families and teachers ought to bear a certain responsibility for our poor behavior. And really, everyone concerned themselves altogether too much with our moral conduct. Later, we were sent to work in the countryside, and there we were very kind and considerate to one another. This, at least, is worth noting. My personal experience can serve as proof: once, during the harvest seasons, I got very sick and thought I was done for. No one came to care for me except for a classmate who was also sick, but who nevertheless half-carried, half-dragged me across the Namwan River to the hospital. Though the river wasn't deep, it was a good five kilometers wide at that time; it had flooded so you couldn't even find the riverbanks. Supposing someone else had become sick, I would have done the same for them. It's things like this that make me think we weren't bad at all, and there was no need to bury ourselves in the countryside and never return, nor to take certain hints and commit mass suicide, making space for the next generation. For all that was good about our character and our behavior, we must thank the teachings of silence.

4

There's one thing that the majority of people know: that we can choose between a culture of discourse and a culture of silence. I've experienced many such opportunities to choose. For example, in the countryside, some of my teammates chose to say a little something, and went to the 'Activists' Congress' to 'share their learning,' expecting to derive some benefit from it. Some of our younger friends may be unfamiliar with these terms, which I'll explain briefly: An Activists' Congress was a Congress of Activists in the Living Study and Implementation of Chairman Mao's Works, and to share one's learnings was to talk about one's experiences and gains in the course of living out Chairman Mao's teachings. Anyone attending the congress was an activist, and to be an activist was a good thing. A further opportunity was – provided you spoke up during the congress and were active in social movements – to become a student cadre, and being a student cadre was also a good thing. I happily passed up both of these opportunities. Now, those who have chosen the culture of speech may not believe that I passed them up of my own accord.

They may think I was simply not a good speaker or didn't make the grade, that I wasn't worthy of speech. Speech is power, and power is yet another good thing, and many people go to great lengths to enter the circles of discourse, even struggling over the 'right to speak.' If I say I willingly gave this up, some will not believe me – fortunately, there are also many who will. My main reason was that, once you've entered these circles, then you must speak their language, you must even use their language to think, and I find this tiresome. As I see it, those circles are mired in anemia.

Twenty years ago I was a sent-down youth* in Yunnan. How the local people viewed us, besides noting that we dressed a little better and had whiter skin, is a complete mystery to me. I believe they thought of us as people standing onstage, and felt they had to speak to us in theatrical language – at least, that's how they thought when we first arrived. This was a mistake, of course, but it was not offensive. A more offensive mistake was that they believed we were all rich and did everything they could to hike the marketplace prices, to the point where we were paying two or three times what the locals paid for every little thing we bought. Later, we learned an unusual trick for shopping: instead of bargaining, we'd toss them a wad of mao bills and let them count it, meanwhile we'd walk

---

* 'Sent-down youth' refers to young people who, beginning in the 1950s and until the end of the Cultural Revolution (1976), were sent from urban to rural areas to work instead of receiving a scholastic education.

off with whatever we wanted to buy. By the time they'd finished counting, both buyer and goods were gone. In the beginning we would give a fair price, but later, some of us gave less and less, even mixing fen in with the mao. Even if I were to proclaim myself innocent, that I'd never done this sort of thing, you'd never believe me, so I'll make no contentions. One day one of the students was finally grabbed by a villager while he was paying like this – of course, I don't mean myself. The villager had made up his mind to thrash the student, but he first stammered and stuttered and at last spat out: 'Hey! No! Mao's Thought, eh? Resist Individualism!' Later, we went home and laughed ourselves into convulsions over what he'd said. These days, as you can imagine, the villager might say something like: 'Hey! No! Four Emphases, eh? Five Beauties!' and we would laugh ourselves to death just the same. I give this example not to take cheap shots or to be clever, but to illustrate the impoverishment of speech. Using it to actually say anything becomes difficult, let alone using it to think.

I passed many years in silence: in the countryside, as a worker, as a college student, and later as a teacher at university. Keeping silent as a teacher sounds impossible, but I taught technical courses and only spoke technical language at the podium, and I vanished as soon as class was out. The way I see it, you can keep silent no matter what it is you do. Of course, I also had a lifelong passion for writing fiction, but I never tried to publish what I wrote, I still maintained my silence. The reasons for this silence are simple: I could

not trust those who belonged to the circles of speech.
The experiences of my short life had taught me that
those circles were nothing but yammering madhouses.
What I doubted then was not just the group that said a
mu of land could produce three hundred thousand jin
of grain and talked about a spiritual atomic bomb – I
doubted all societies of speech. If you could prove to
me today that I'd mistakenly committed a grave gen-
eralization, my happy relief would know no bounds.

5

You may not believe me when I say I kept silent for so
many years; you weren't born yesterday, after all. You
don't believe that I've never 'stated my position' during a
meeting; that I have never written a criticism, and you'd
be right to doubt: I can prove neither that I am mute
nor that I am illiterate, and in truth I have done both the
stating and the criticizing. By my standards, however,
none of that is real speech, but instead the payment of a
kind of speech tax. We've heard that, in years past, even
great people sometimes 'spoke contrary to their own
hearts,' and thus we can see that the tax is applied very
broadly indeed. Because of the speech tax we cannot be
held responsible for everything that we have said: our
superiors made us say it. But if all speech is only a payment of tax, then we're in trouble. What can all that
speech be used for? It's talk, not money. It can't be used
to build dams, nor power stations. Once paid, it can only
be left there to rot, to be mocked by future generations.

Of course, I shouldn't concern myself about the uses of expropriated speech; perhaps it has other functions I've not thought of. What I want to say is, the collection of the speech tax has been going on since ancient times. Those who speak have always known of the need to pay it. That need has been absorbed into their blood, and realized in their mouths.

There's an example of this in the classic Chinese novel *The Story of the Stone*, in which two young girls are playing a game of poetic free-association in the garden. Line follows after line, and eventually out comes something from the ancient *Book of Songs.* It was discouraging to read: a couple of teenage girls, in their own backyard in the middle of the night, and still they feel obliged to quote *The Book of Songs*. Unpacking this a little more carefully, of course, it's the author who has the real problem: the unshakeable compulsion, when speaking, to pay the speech tax. I believe that the world of speech varies between two extremes. At one extreme is the speech of sages, which is freely given. At the other is the speech of the silent, which is coin levied by force. All speech between these two extremes is difficult to resolve: it is both an offering, and an appropriation. There is a tax official in the hearts of all those who speak. Chinese scholars have a very strong sense

---

* *The Book of Songs* is the oldest of the Chinese classics, a collection of 305 songs dating back over two thousand years to the Zhou dynasty. They are considered the basis of Confucianism and later of Chinese literature.

of their obligation to society, but this is only speech taxation, it is being a good taxpayer. That may be an ugly way of putting it; a better way would be to say they take the troubles of the world upon their shoulders.

I once was a silent person, meaning that I did not like to speak in meetings, nor to write articles. Recently, this much has changed: I'll speak during meetings, and occasionally write a little something. I have had a strong reaction to this change, and feel as though I lost my childhood innocence. It means betraying years of long-standing practice; that I no longer belong to the silent majority. This not only causes me pain, but also a faint sense of depression. The resumption of speech does not mean the resumption of my tax-paying responsibilities – if that were the case, I would be nothing but a giant basket of nonsense. My responsibilities lie elsewhere.

A few years ago, I participated in some sociological research and thus came into contact with some marginalized groups, the most unusual of these being homosexuals. After doing this research, I suddenly realized: the so-called minority groups were simply groups whose speech went unsaid. Because they had not spoken out, other people thought they didn't exist, or were very distant. People still don't believe that homosexuals exist in China. Abroad, people know homosexuals exist, but don't know who they are. Two scholars in the humanities wrote a book entitled *Word is Out*. Later, I had another sudden understanding: that I belonged to the greatest disadvantaged group in history, the silent majority. These people keep silent for any number of reasons, some because they lack the ability or the opportunity to speak, others because they are hiding something, and still others because they feel, for whatever reason, a certain distaste for the world of speech. I am one of these last groups and, as one of them, I have a duty to speak of what I have seen and heard.

6

Most of what I write falls into the category of literature. In my opinion, so-called literature should go like this: just write well, and to hell with the rest of it. I can think of nowhere but literature where my odd ideas would fit in. Blame literature for giving me a foothold within this circle; a foothold from which I can attack the circle itself, and attack the entire world of the yang.

A few years ago, I was studying in America. Someone there once asked me: You Chinese people talk about yin and yang; how come all good things belong to the yang, and nothing good is left for the yin? This is because the right to speak belongs to the yang, so, of course, it will have nothing good to say about the yin. Confucius himself couldn't avoid this convention, and attacked 'women and people of mean character' as a lump. This phrase of his has been repeated for thousands of years, but I have never heard a single response from the subjects of the attack. Everyone takes pains not to be seen as a person of mean character, but no one has yet resolved the question of how not to be a woman. Even in this modern age, female-to-male sex change operations are a point of contention. Put simply, the things that are said in the circles of speech will never meet with rebuttal. You could be charitable and call this 'saying one's piece'; it could be described less charitably with a popular phrase describing immoral behavior: 'Beating the deaf, cursing the mute, and trampling on graves.' But I know one fact for absolute certain: anyone who speaks will do so imperfectly, even saints will speak imperfectly, and these imperfections are not trivial.

By now I have also wormed my way into the circles of speech, and this can only mean one thing: those circles are already crumbling. In light of this unfortunate truth, there have been many calls to action: We must shore up China's spiritual structure, and so forth. As someone originally from a different circle, I have a suggestion for my friends in this new one: Let us examine ourselves. Have we become stupid? Have we become mad? There are many mirrors that can be used for self-examination: Chinese tradition is one, foreign culture is another. Another, even larger mirror is right by our side – the silent majority. All this is simply spoken from the heart, of course. A few years ago, when I had just emerged from silence, I wrote a book and gave it to someone I respected. He didn't like the book, he thought that books weren't supposed to be like that. In his view, books should educate the people, and elevate their souls – and these words are worth their weight in gold. But among all the people of the world, the one I wish most to elevate is myself. This is contemptible; it is selfish; it is also true.

The Maverick Pig

At the commune, I fed pigs and herded oxen. Had there not been anyone around to manage them, those two animals would have known exactly how to live. They would have wandered around eating and drinking as they pleased, and when spring came they would have looked for a little romance. Of course, in such a scenario, their standard of living would have been very low; it would have been totally unremarkable. Then, people came along who sought to give their lives a little more purpose: every ox and every pig was given a livelihood. For the majority of them, these livelihoods were quite tragic: the former's was to work and the latter's was to grow meat. I don't really consider this something worth complaining about because my life at the time wasn't much more interesting than that. Aside from the eight featured model operas, I didn't have any other entertainment. Then, there were the minority of pigs and oxen whose lives had a different purpose. Take pigs, for example – boars and sows had other things to do in addition to eating. But from what I could tell, they weren't particularly thrilled about the arrangement either. The boar's purpose was to breed. In other words, our policy allowed for them to be studs. But the weary boar often put on an air of propriety that was usually reserved for meat pigs (meat pigs are castrated), and refused to jump on the sow's back. The sow's purpose was to rear the young, but some of the sows ended up eating their own piglets. In short, human management has made pigs as miserable as can be. But they still accepted it: pigs are pigs after all.

Managing every aspect of life is something of a specialty among humans. Not only animals, but they also like to manage themselves. I know that in ancient Greece, there was Sparta where they managed themselves into absolute bores. The purpose was to turn the men into intrepid warriors and the women into reproductive machines. The former became like fighting cocks and the latter became sows. These are very interesting species indeed, but my impression was that they didn't much like their lives. But so what if they didn't like it? Whether it be human or animal, it is very hard to change one's own fate.

The following is the story of a pig who was unlike the rest. When I started feeding it, it was around four or five years of age. Nominally, it was a meat pig. It was long and black and lean with a pair of bright shining eyes. The fellow was as agile as a mountain goat, easily leaping over the meter-tall pig fence; it could even jump onto the roof of the barn, a bit like a cat in that regard – which was why it was able to roam around all the time and hardly spend any time in the pigsty. All the intellectual youths who fed pigs treated it like a pet, and it was my pet too – because it only got along with intellectual youths, allowing only us to get within three meters of it;

had it been anyone else, it would have run. It was a male, it should have been castrated. But if you tried, even if you hid the hog knife behind your back, it would have been able to smell it. It would have stared at you with its big eyes and grunted ferociously. I always fed the rice bran porridge to it first; only when it had eaten enough did I mix the rest with weeds to feed the other pigs. The other pigs would get jealous and become rowdy. The entire farm wailed and howled but the pig and I didn't care. When it had filled up its belly, it would jump on the roof or try to imitate different sounds. It knew how to make a car noise and a tractor noise, all very convincingly; sometimes when it vanished for days, I assumed it had gone to look for sows in the nearby villages. We had sows here too, locked up in the pigsty where excessive farrowing had left their bodies misshapen. They were also dirty and smelly. It wasn't interested in them; the village sows were better looking. It left behind all sorts of tales but my time feeding pigs was short so my knowledge of them is limited, which is why I won't bother relating them all here. In short, all the intellectual youths who fed it loved it. They loved its unapologetic attitude and the way it lived life to the fullest. The country folks weren't quite as romantic. They said, the pig was deviant. The leadership hated it, a point which I will come back to. My feeling for it was beyond love – I respected it, so much so that I ignored the fact that I was more than a dozen years older than it and called it 'big brother pig.' As was mentioned, this brother pig was able to imitate sounds. I assume it had tried to speak like a human, but wasn't able to learn – had it been successful, we would have poured our hearts out to each other. But it couldn't be blamed. The vocal ranges of pigs and humans simply differ too much.

Later, brother pig learned to make a steam whistle sound, which led to some problems. Nearby was a sugar factory that blew its steam whistle once before noon when the workers changed shifts. Every day at ten in the morning, my pig brother would jump on the roof and imitate the steam whistle. When the people in the field heard it, they returned – this was an hour and a half before the sugar factory was supposed to blow its whistle. To be frank, this wasn't entirely brother pig's fault; after all, it wasn't a kettle and the sound it made differed from that of the steam whistle in important ways, but the folks insisted they couldn't tell the difference. The leadership convened a meeting where they labeled it a counter-revolutionary who was ruining spring planting; they needed to take authoritarian measures – that was basically the spirit of the meeting, but I wasn't worried for it – because if by *authoritarian*, they meant ropes and hog knives, then that would not even get them out the door. It wasn't as if the previous leadership had not tried, a hundred men couldn't catch it. Dogs were no use: brother pig ran like a torpedo, easily knocking a dog back a yard or more. But this time, they upped the ante. The political instructor led twenty some men, armed with all sorts of handguns; the vice instructor led over a dozen, armed with old-fashioned muskets, and they went out in two groups to hunt the pig in the clearing behind the farm. My heart was conflicted: considering the bond we had, I should have charged out with two hog knives and stood shoulder to shoulder with it to the end, but I realized that in doing so, I would have been upturning tradition – after all, it was only a pig; another reason was that I didn't have the courage to rebel against the leadership; I suspect that was more of where the problem was. Anyway, I watched from the sideline. Brother pig's serenity won my total admiration: it calmly hid in between both the handguns' and muskets' lines of fires; no matter how much people yelled and dogs barked, it never left that center line. This way, if the men with handguns fired, they would kill the men with muskets, and vice versa; if both sides fired at the same time, they would have all died. As for it, it was small enough that it would probably have been fine. Like that, it went around in circles until it found an opening and charged through; it ran with abandon. After that, I only saw it one more time among the sugarcane. It had grown tusks. It still recognized me, but it didn't let me get close anymore. Its reticence broke my heart, but I support its desire to keep a distance with those who bore sinister intentions toward it.

I am forty years old now. Other than this pig, I have yet to see anyone with such a total disregard for the life that was set out for them. On the contrary, I have seen many people who try to manage other people's lives and many people who are fine with letting their lives be managed. For that reason, I continue to reminisce on this pig who went its own way.

War in the Belly

Once when I was young, I got sick and had to stay in the hospital. At the time, there weren't any doctors in the hospital, only members of the worker and peasant army turned health workers – all the real doctors were sent to remote areas to be reeducated in the ways of the lower- and middle-peasant class. On the other hand, what else would you call someone wearing a white gown but 'doctor'? During my first day at the hospital, a doctor came to look at my test results, then listened to me all over with a stethoscope, and finally asked: what's your disease? Of course he didn't understand the test results. But even without a test you could tell what I had: my whole body was the color of day-old tea: I had jaundice. I told him, by my own estimation, that I had hepatitis. This incident happened twenty years ago and at the time, we had never heard of hepatitis B, much less hepatitis C, D, and E. There was just the one infectious hepatitis. Apparently, hepatitis didn't exist in China until the three-year famine[*]

[*] The Great Chinese Famine was a period from 1959 to 1961, widely considered to be one of the deadliest famines in history. It was one of the greatest man-made disasters of the

when people started to eat Iraqi jujubes – they called it jujube but it was really a palm date. Even though I had never eaten a palm date, I still got the disease. The doctor asked me what to do. I said, why don't you just give me some vitamins – that's how my disease was cured. To be honest, staying at the hospital did nothing to help my condition, but I still thought it was better for me to stay there. At least that way I wouldn't infect anyone else in my troop.

At the hospital, there weren't any distractions so the only thing there was to do was to watch the doctors perform surgery on people. The knife was always aimed at the appendix – at least they knew enough to know to not mess with any more complicated procedures. I'm not kidding when I say I watched surgeries. At the time, there often wasn't electricity and what electrical supply there was, wasn't stable. The surgeries were performed in a room with four glass walls. The sunlight was best at two in the afternoon so that's when they did the surgery – all the patients at the hospital could watch and bet on how many hours it would take to find the appendix. Later when I told my friends at the medical university about this, they didn't believe me. They said, are you sure an appendectomy can take several hours? You can choose to believe me or not, but of the surgeries I saw, never once did they find the appendix in under an hour. The ones who performed the surgery complained,

---

20th century, resulting from policies associated with the Great Leap Forward (1958–1962).

the human appendix is too hard to find – several of them were trained as horse and mule veterinarians, and had experienced performing surgery on army horses. Horse appendices are large and mule appendices aren't small either; they are all larger than human appendices. Even when taking into consideration relative proportions, human appendices are small. When we were chatting during breaks, I said to them: if you're not familiar with human plumbing, then maybe you shouldn't perform surgery on humans. You know what they said? 'The more unfamiliar we are, the more we have to do it – the battlefield is the best learning place!' Young people today may not be familiar with the words but the second half of the sentence came from the *Quotations from Chairman Mao*. Human organs and warfare aren't the same thing, but no one bothered to point that out. There was one thing that I found even more disgusting: every time they performed a surgery, they had someone new try it. That way everyone could learn on the so-called battlefield, and the appendix could never be found. Where the knife landed and how big to make the cut were all a matter of personal preference. But there is at least one nice thing I can say about them: even though some of the cuts veered left, some veered right, and some even hit the mark, at least all the cuts landed on the belly. We should be thankful for that.

At the hospital, I met a guy who had appendicitis. The doctor urged him to undergo surgery. I told him not to do it under any circumstance – if there was no other option, he should request for me to do it. Even though I had never studied medicine, I once fixed an alarm clock and even one of our troops' hand-crank radios. Those two feats alone made me more qualified than any of the doctors at the hospital. Perhaps it was bad luck on his part, but after opening his belly, they spent three hours and still couldn't find his appendix. The doctor panicked and pulled out all his entrails to rummage through. When I was a kid, there was a breakfast spot near my house that sold fried livers and braised intestines. Every day, at the break of dawn, the chef would be outside washing pork intestines. That's what it reminded me of. The sky was starting to dim so more helping hands joined in the search. My man got tired of waiting so he pulled the white curtain aside and looked for his appendix himself. Finally, just before the sun set beyond the mountain, they found it and cut it off. The sky turned black. Had they been a bit slower, it would have been too dark to see and he would have had to spend the night with his guts hanging out. Before that, my favorite dish in the world had been pork intestines; after watching that surgery, I have never wanted to eat any again.

It's been almost thirty years. The reason why I am suddenly reminded of watching other people's surgeries at the hospital is because I am still shocked by how confused people were back then; they may as well have been insane. Who knows, maybe in thirty years, looking back at the people and things today, it will look like we are insane too. In that respect, it seems like every thirty years, our level of rationality takes a qualitative leap forward – but I suspect this theory won't hold up. If rationality can advance in leaps like that, that's basically like saying people before us weren't rational. Take the events of thirty years ago for example, the wielder of the surgical blade held a living man's guts in his dirty hands and rummaged through it. Even though he said he was learning on the battlefield, I still think he knew it was all buffoonery. Therefore, I come to this conclusion: of all the absurdities in human affairs, even though historical background plays a role, it is usually not the deciding factor. The deciding factor is this: the person making a farce of things is opportunistically monkeying around. That is to say, he knew what he did was absurd but he did it anyway because it was fun.

We can push the inference even further: no matter what society is like, people need to take responsibility for their own actions – but for the writer of the essay to lay out his point so nakedly is a bit embarrassing, so I will stop. My story about my hospital stay isn't finished just yet: as I stayed at the hospital, my hepatitis wasn't getting any better; my face got yellower and yellower; my man who underwent surgery couldn't get his cut to heal so he also got skinnier and skinnier. We partnered up and returned to Beijing to seek treatment. I got better the moment I came back but my man ended up back in the hospital for another procedure. The doctor in Beijing said, even though the appendix was removed, his intestine wasn't stitched up properly. The end of it fused to the cut on his belly and formed a fistula. The contents of the intestine were leaking out so the cut could never heal. The doctor added that it was fortunate the contents leaked outward and not back into the stomach or else he would have died. But my man didn't feel so fortunate. He said: damn, no wonder I'm always hungry, everything was leaking. My man certainly was generous. Had that not been the case, he certainly wouldn't have offered his own innards for others to learn how to battle.

Thinking and Feeling Ashamed

As a young man I was stationed at a commune in Yunnan. The place had still been considered part of the savage outskirts of China only a few decades prior. For that reason, in addition to verdant mountains and pristine waters, the local culture was also pure and humble. When I was there, in addition to working the land, the local people also had another exhausting task: to present themselves as sophisticated people. Back then, at the beginning of every meeting, one had to say some trendy phrases to come off as an intellectual. This was easy for us, but for the old country folks it was a challenge. For example, when our captain wanted to offer some words about the work going on in the fields – which for him as a seasoned ploughman should have been a piece of cake – he had to start with some sort of fashionable phrase, and that stumped him. Judging from his quivering lips, he seemed to be about to say, 'Down with private interest and bourgeois revisionism,' a simple phrase, not difficult to utter – that is, for those like us, it was mighty hard for him. His face turned red as he swallowed one word after the next. Sweat beads the size of peas rolled down his cheeks, but he still couldn't squeeze out the phrase. In the end, what came out was: fuck it, there's more than one way to run a farm! After hearing his brilliant rendition, we rose up in applause. I like simple people and I think he spoke just fine. But he had a higher standard in mind for himself because he wanted to sound sophisticated.

They say that in the olden times in Poland, when country women from a certain village met each other on the road, the first thing they said was always, 'the Saint Mother Mary may be praised'; when someone from another village heard this, they scratched their head and said, 'Yeah, she could be praised, so why don't you praise her?' Such an interpretation misses the point. The point wasn't to praise Mother Mary but to show one's sophistication. Back in the day, when we used to start every sentence with 'the prime directive says,' it was for the same reason. In *The Dream of the Red Chamber*,* when Lin Daiyu and Shi Xiangyun are in the garden playing literary domino, suddenly a verse praising the queen mother pops out. The author probably thought that since Lin was an educated elite, she should speak with sophistication. As for our captain, he was after the same affect but he wasn't as eloquent as sister Lin. For some reason, trendy phrases made him feel so ashamed that he couldn't get them out of his mouth for the life of him;

---

* *The Story of Stone* counts among the four great classical novels of Chinese literature. Written by Cao Xueqin in the mid-eighteenth century, it is also called *The Dream of a Red Chamber*. Divided into five volumes, it charts the glory and decline of the illustrious Jia family and is known for its psychological scope and its observations of Chinese society at the time.

whatever came out inevitably included a couple of swear words. As a result, all the male intellectual youths fell in love with him. Before every meeting, we would wait in silent anticipation. The moment he spoke, we rose in applause, which only made his problem get worse.

Once, our troop was playing a basketball game against another troop, and he was our team leader – you wouldn't believe it if I told you, our captain knew how to play basketball. Even though he wasn't a great player, he was always able to make sure the other team sustained injuries. Sometimes there was blood on a chest, sometimes there were swollen gonads; he was an impressive center, our victory depended on his fierceness – the two teams lined up on the basketball court. The captain from the other team read from the *Quotations from Chairman Mao*. Then, it was his turn. He managed to speak without any swear words, which was disappointing to those of us who were eager to applaud. Who would have guessed that the captain ended up getting a whistle blown viciously at him by the referee. He was berated: the highest order is the highest order and revolutionary slogans are revolutionary slogans, you can't mix them up! He was then taken off the court where he sat to a side with a green face. As it turned out, what he said was: the prime directive says, long live Chairman Mao! The referee felt that the sentence was incorrect. The prime directive refers to the things Chairman Mao said. The venerable old man never said 'long live' to himself. So his words were indeed incorrect. But I didn't think there was reason to correct simple people, your own sophistication should have been enough. After having gotten the whistle blown at him, our captain never dared to speak again, with or without swear words. He practically became a mute . . .

All the trendy phrases back then basically said the same thing, which was 'be loyal and obey authority' – that's not a secret; back then, everyone lionized loyalty. Yet even though the words were the same, some people felt ashamed to say them while others didn't. That's where the subtlety lies. The ones who felt ashamed weren't necessarily less loyal or obedient. Take our captain for example, he was actually the most loyal, obedient player on the team. But his sense of loyalty and obedience came from a feeling deep in his heart. It was almost a rather feminine attitude. It wasn't just obedience and loyalty but love. That was why he wasn't willing to lay it all out in public in that corny way. Our captain's loyalty was evident in his willingness to work hard and plant good crops; but to ask him to stand in public and talk about it was putting him on the spot. A good analogy would be dating. Some men like to show love through their actions and not say 'I love you' too loudly. Our captain was one of those. Other kinds of people didn't feel that way so they could say those things without feeling corny; but that by no means meant they were more loyal or obedient in their hearts – similarly, some studs will say 'I love you' with their every breath, but you don't really know if their love is real.

As I mentioned, the place where I was stationed had a pure and humble culture. The locals felt it was embarrassing to display their simplicity in public; as a result, being sophisticated became synonymous with feeling ashamed. It wasn't only the captain who felt this way, just about everyone did. The following is an illustration from my personal experience: once I was at the farmer's market buying things. The thing I wanted to buy was a jackfruit from this old Dai lady.* One thing I need to clarify is that at the time, the locals all thought that all intellectual youths were rich. They upcharged us such that we paid two to three times what the locals paid for everything. That was why when we bought things, we waited until the vendor wasn't paying attention, then threw down the correct amount of money, grabbed the item, and ran. Some people call this way of buying things stealing, but I didn't think so – of course, I no longer buy things in this way. That day, I didn't have enough money on me so the amount of money I threw down wasn't quite enough. The old Dai lady – or as the locals say, *mieba* – came chasing after me, yelling and screaming. She yelled: 'No way! So sophisticated! Down with private ownership and bourgeois revisionism . . .' and in my moment of weakness, the said jackfruit – also called cow belly fruit – was stolen back. As you now know, when this *mieba* said those sophisticated phrases, what she meant was: you should be ashamed of yourself! Those words really hit home, even now when I think about it, I still feel embarrassed: just for a bite of a cow belly fruit, I was called a sophisticated thinker. Oh, the shame.

* The Dai are an ethnic minority native to China's Yunnan province. Their language is related to the Thai and Laotian languages.

Concerning 'the Greatness Tribe'

An old classmate of mine returned from America to visit his family. We had not seen each other for almost eight years. He's not doing poorly: even though his salary isn't very high, he lives comfortably in a two-income household. Since last seeing him in America, he's moved on to his third home, upgraded to his fourth car, and as far as PC computers are concerned, the moment a newer, faster one comes out, he runs to buy it, so you can't keep track of how many of those have passed through his hands. He hasn't upgraded his wife yet, and isn't planning to, which is the part I like about him. Even though he hasn't ridden in a Rolls-Royce or stayed in a mansion on Palm Beach, and even though he doesn't hold a stack of stocks in his hands, only a buttload of debt, still, as we like to say in the Northeast, at least he has 'spent' a good time. Right now, I am without a roof or a plot of land to my name, so of course, I am a little envious. But when we got together, this was not what we talked about – that would have been far too inane.

This brother and I have ventured in all four directions. We've farmed the land, herded livestock, worked in factories, and twenty years ago when we shared the same window in college, our hearts burned with the same fiery ambition, and together, we dreamed of accomplishing great things. By great things, I just mean making our dreams come true. As for what we dreamed about, I'm too embarrassed to mention now, so I'll just use other people's dreams as examples. Take the big boss of the Microsoft Corporation, Bill Gates – for example, when he was young, he wanted to take the unassuming little microprocessor of his day and turn it into a useful computer that everyone could own and use, ushering in a scientific era that would truly sweep across mankind – that's the stuff great dreams are made of. Today, this dream has largely come true, and he has made a significant contribution to that progress, truly admirable. But as for his business success, that seems less admirable to me. Another example would be Martin Luther King Jr who once declared 'I have a dream,' and now on American campuses, you can see Black boys and girls strolling along with white boys and girls. From such a beautiful image, one can sense the greatness of Dr King's dream. But fast-forward to the present, there's not much more for me to add, and my cheeks are starting to get hot. All I can say is that we once had these kinds of dreams too.

Every person has his or her own dream, but such dreams aren't always the start of something great. Mr Lu Xun once wrote about a certain kind of person in his essay: his biggest dream was to cough up half a mouthful of blood on a snowy day and have his maid support him as he lazily ambled into the courtyard to enjoy the plum blossoms. When I read this, it made me furious:

how can someone have a dream like that! At the time, I thought: if this old mister wasn't so particular about the snow, the plum blossoms, the maid, and just wanted to cough up some blood, then that's something I could help him with. At the time, I was a young man with muscles on my arms and a hard fist. Nowadays, I wouldn't offer this sort of help. I'm past that age. Now, when I look in the mirror and see a wrinkly face, I hardly recognize the person. When I'm walking on the street and come across a colossal object that upon closer inspection turns out to be the girl of my dreams from back in the day, I can't help but swallow a mouthful of cold air. When you swallow too much cold air, you start to forget things, so I should get all I have to say off my chest while I still can. Not every dream is the start of something great, but all great things start from a dream – of that I am certain.

Young people today have their 'celebrity fan tribes' and 'office worker tribes,' but the ones who want to achieve greatness don't have a name so let's call them the 'greatness tribe.' Back in the day, campuses (whether it was in China or America) were full of these types. When Mr Gates showed up on campus with his casual wear and a head full of messy hair, he was just like us, a part of the 'greatness tribe.' When I first got back to China, at least half of the students I taught belonged to the greatness tribe. Their eyes sparkled with the dream of greatness. I could always tell with one glance who was or wasn't a part of the tribe. But this tribe has gotten smaller and smaller, and one day, maybe they will go extinct like the dinosaurs. I asked this brother of mine, what are you doing these days. He said he sat around and helped people run software packages. I yelled at him in anger: people like us should be doing research – who wants to run software packages? But he said, they pay me, so who cares. It made sense. If someone paid me thirty or forty thousand American dollars a year to run software packages, I'd run his packages too. This shows that even I am no longer a part of the greatness tribe. But when we were young, we had grand dreams. The greatness tribe isn't a bunch of daydreamers, nor are they just loud voices in an angry mob; and they certainly aren't teenagers whose blood rises to a boil before they've even figured out what's going on. The greatness tribe believes that all beautiful dreams can come true – in other words, dreams that can't come true aren't beautiful to begin with. If you don't succeed, then you must have done something wrong; and if you succeed and the results aren't beautiful, but more like a nightmare, then you must have thought about it wrong to begin with. No matter how it turns out, this road must always exist – prepare a dream and prepare to work toward that dream. Whether or not this way of thinking is correct, I'm not yet certain. One thing I am sure about is: there exists a greatness tribe.

The Feeling of Domestic Product and Cultural Relativism

In *The Water Margin*, Song Jiang broke the law and was stabbed, then exiled to the River Lands under the charge of Dai Zong. Customarily, he should have offered Dai Zong some sort of a bribe, but he refused to do so. As a result, Dai Zong had to ask Song Jiang to bribe him. Song Jiang still refused and questioned: 'You are in no possession of some shortcoming of mine, what right do you have to ask me for ransom?' Dai Zong was furious: 'How dare you question my right! You are a prisoner in my charge; I can construe even your coughing as a crime! You, fellow, are a piece of line product in my hands!' Domestic products mean shabby products. Dai Zong compares Song Jiang to a cheap item and himself to the proprietor of said item. I was twenty years old when I first read this story. Ever since then, I have been unable to shake off the feeling of being a piece of domestic ware or product. It is a tragic feeling. In this Eastern society I inhabit, there is nothing that can soothe my woe – this feeling of sadness does not derive from the literal facts of my existence, but from the unfortunate reality of domestic product – with which I feel affinity – itself. The thing that tells you you are a piece of domestic product is this: no matter what people decide to do with you, and no matter how they evaluate you, they don't need to offer an explanation or ask for your consent. I once had such an experience: when I was seventeen, I was suddenly put on a train and shipped off to Yunnan. On my body was a label that read: HARROWER OF THE HINTERLAND. To this I offer no protest; I only have this burning feeling of being a piece of domestic product. In the Chinese cultural tradition, there is an explanation: 'Under all of heaven, not all land belongs to the king; between the water's margins, not all land belongs to the duke. . . .' It's true that under all of heaven, not all the land belongs to the king; I'm not the king; between the water's margins, not all land belongs to the duke; I'm still not the king. To me, it would have been more direct if they had just said that I was a piece of domestic product.

The ancient Egyptians thought that the Earth is round – as you know, that's the truth; the ancient Greeks, though, thought the Earth was a flat board resting on the back of a giant whale. The whale drifted in the sea and when the whale got a back itch, it would scratch it, and you would have an earthquake – that's not the truth. Bertrand Russell pointed out that this wasn't because the Egyptians were smart and the Greeks were dumb. The Egyptians lived in a wide-open terrain. A look around revealed a curved horizon. It wasn't hard for them to reach the right conclusion. The Greeks lived in a mountainous coastline with frequent earthquakes. It is no wonder they thought about seas and whales. Identical people will have different understandings of their relationship to the environment depending on whether they live in an open terrain or in the mountains. If a person is born a piece of domestic product, their understanding will inevitably be different from someone born a proprietor of goods. An example of the latter perspective would be America's Declaration of Independence. This was written two hundred years ago by a group of North American plantation owners. By our standards, the document is full of brazen violations. As for examples of the former, the Chinese classics are full of them, starting from Confucius. Compared to the Declaration of Independence, they are full of domestic jargon. I am unsatisfied with their discourse and plan to offer my criticism. But I need a platform to stand on: I have to prove that I'm not a piece of product – as such, it is not proper to criticize the proprietor of products.

In recent years, cultural fever shows no signs of diminution. Western theories surge into China wave after wave. Some of these theories with Western origins are the stuff of my nightmares – these include cultural relativism, functionalism, etc., that said, culture is a tool for living (Malinowski's functional theory), no culture is any worse than any other (cultural relativism), and other nightmares. In principle, these perspectives are correct, but everything depends on how to apply them. In the hands of a crook, any good idea can be spoiled. Take for example Song Jiang in the River Lands prison. He lives within a special kind of culture (let's call it Song dynasty prison culture). According to the rules of this culture, he is a product in the hands of Dai Zong, he should offer Dai Zong some perks. If he says to Dai Zong, all men are equal and I am a man, so why do you call me domestic product? There is something wrong with this culture. Dai Zong can then say: Song Jiang, according to the principle of cultural relativism, there's nothing wrong with any culture. Our culture is fine just the way it is, so you should simply accept being my domestic product. Song Jiang might reply: perhaps the culture is fine, but for you to ask me for perks is an act of blackmail, I can't oblige. Dai Zong can then say: culture is a tool for living. If in our culture, you have to offer me perks, then there must be some function being served. Therefore, you should just offer me something. If you don't, then I will have to act in accordance with our culture and beat you with a stick – don't worry, beating you has its function too. This example shows that cultural anthropology cannot stand up to Dai Zong's misuse and abuse. In truth, no science can stand up to misuse and abuse. But there are some scholars who study Western sciences precisely to distort them using traditional Eastern thought. Using cultural relativism, they can indeed squeeze out the logic that we are all domestic products.

As we know, in Africa there is a custom of female circumcision, leaving scars on the female body and mind. Some African women are ready to fight to resist this practice. Suppose there are people in Africa who despise Western theories, they could say: this is our culture, you can't touch it. They might even bring up cultural relativism and offer a bunch of nonsense. Cultural relativism enables anthropologists to look at other cultures respectfully. It's not there to prove that Song Jiang is a domestic product, nor is it there to support female circumcision in Africa. So long as a person lives under the influence of their own culture, they have the right to criticize that culture. I offer criticism to the culture which I inhabit because I live here, under the influence of this culture. Suppose I got a green card and lived overseas and you said I didn't have the right, I would have to concede. A person should be the master of his own fate, not someone else's domestic product. If you can't even understand that, then you may as well be a walking corpse, and walking corpses don't have the right to talk science.

Culture Wars

In Bertrand Russell's *Power: A New Social Analysis*, he mentions the concept of clerical power, which was once wielded by the clergy. He adds, in the West, intellectuals are the heirs of the clerical class. In addition, Russell states that in China, Confucian scholars also wield clerical power. That leads one to assume that in China, intellectuals are the heirs of Confucian scholars. Clerics and Confucians possess knowledge derived from sacred texts, the Holy Bible, the Analects, and such. Yet modern intellectuals, for the most part, do not carry around sacred texts. Their persuasiveness derives entirely from knowledge; a type of knowledge that is inherently persuasive. But the funny thing is the latter form of knowledge does not bring with it power.

Placing Confucianism side by side with religions will inevitably invite controversy. Confucianism does not adopt the name of God, nor does it use heaven and hell to scare people. But it, too, relies on a mythology, which is that without it, people will have no ability to govern. Chaos will reign under heaven. Order, ethics, morality will all be gone. This mythology has intimidated generation after generation of Chinese people. Even now, some people believe it. Russell states that people's deference toward scholars never comes from an understanding of truth but from the magic that they imagine the experts possess. I believe that the magic of Confucianism is precisely the myth of governance. Of course, based on its content, Confucianism is a type of philosophy, but the words of the sages contain only conclusions and judgments, while they lack in evidence and logic. Without considering its myth about governance, its conclusions would not be very convincing.

When Russell talks about 'truth,' he is talking about science. This is a type of knowledge that can be acquired by anyone with normal mental capacities if they are willing to put in the work. As is well known, science cannot solve all problems, especially when it comes to value judgments. As such, some people consider it shallow. However, if you only spent some time studying it, you would find that it is very different from Confucianism.

We understand that the foundation of Confucian learning is memorization. One must remember every single sentence uttered by the sage. I believe that if Confucius and Meng-tzu came back to life and saw how their descendants continue to repeat their words, they would find it strange. Of course, not all students of Confucianism are merely record players. After all, they add their own phrase before the sage's words, namely, 'Confucius says.' Such an absurd phenomenon reveals the spirit of Confucian learning: to become copies of the sage. This copying process takes the form of memorization. On the other hand, one could also believe that these Confucian scholars have another motive. As we know, some people use the *Merriam-Webster's Dictionary* to study English. Compared to memorizing the books of the sage, memorizing the dictionary imparts almost no material advantage. Suppose you were able to become the sage's copy, then you would possess the magic of governance. You could show your meritocratic credentials and be elevated into officialdom; but memorizing the *Merriam-Webster Dictionary* will only qualify you to be a translator and earn you twenty yuan per a thousand words. These two exercises in memorization cannot even be mentioned in the same breath.

Now let us look at science. Its complexity aside, it is something that one agrees with as soon as one understands it. It is different from the idea that 'rulers rule, administrators administrate, parents parent, kids kid' and different from 'the unity of heaven and man.' I've known these two sentences for many years and still don't agree with them. More importantly, science doesn't encourage scholars to become the clones of certain paradigms, nor does it claim to have some sort of magic. Because our Western intellectual counterparts brought up this idea, they no longer enjoy the deference they once did. If we believe what Mr Russell is saying, Western intellectuals basically blew their own gig. Regrettably, they didn't only blow their own gig but they also blew the gigs of Chinese intellectuals too. Even more regrettably, there are some Chinese intellectuals who want to blow our own gigs as well – yours truly being one of them.

Ever since the beginning of modernity, people have been debating about the merits of traditional culture.

We know that culture is the way people live, it is multi-faceted. But the debates over tradition have always taken place at the level of philosophy, which is why the term *culture war* is not very fitting. In this debate, it is always mentioned that China's situation is unique. In my view, one side of the debate is always hinting at the magic of traditional governance, implying that China cannot be divorced from this magical force. If my understanding is correct, talking about divorcing China from this magical force actually involves two distinct issues. One is whether the descendants of Confucian officialdom can be divorced from this magical force. The other is whether China's proletarian masses can be divorced from this magical force. To mix the two issues together is clearly inappropriate. Taken separately, the first question should be simple to answer. After having lost the myth of governance, the descendants of the Confucian officialdom, even if they find careers as professors and researchers, do not enjoy a status comparable to that of their ancestors. In relation to this phenomenon, Mr Russell has something like the following to say: 'When intellectuals found that their prestige has suffered as a result of their own activities, they began to feel resentment toward the modern world.' There, he was talking about the situation in the West. In China, the sentence should be rephrased as: when Chinese intellectuals found that their prestige suffered because of the activities of Western intellectuals, they began to hate Western learning and foreigners in general. As for the second issue, the more you think about it, the harder it is to make the case. I have always suspected that people are thinking about the first issue while talking about the second. To be honest, I wish my suspicions were unwarranted.

We know that successful generals always pick their battles. For generals to be strategic is a good thing, but whether it is good for scholars to be strategic is another question. Those who support traditional culture have a theory that all tribes need to respect their own cultural tradition, or else there is no future for them. It is the opinion of yours truly that such a line of reasoning raises the suspicion of being overly strategic. On the battlefield of tradition, Confucians have more to gain than other people. Non-Confucians have every reason to avoid such a challenge. Not long ago, yours truly participated in a debate. In this debate, some men wanted to return to the traditional arrangement where men rule outside the home and women rule inside the home; several women participants disagreed. Clearly, on the battlefield of tradition, men have more to gain than women. Even though I am a man, I stood on the side of women; it was because I hate these underhanded tactics.

Now let us return to the main point. Mr Russell once said that he supported the idea of universal equality. But unfortunately, reality is never quite like that. People are not equal, especially when it comes to their knowledge. With differential knowledge comes power. Suppose that everyone in the world was ignorant and there was only one person who was omniscient, that person would easily acquire power. Traditional Chinese sages thirsted for knowledge at least as much as modern scientists. As far as I know, the sage Zhu Xi had a lust for learning second to none in history. The difference between scientists and sages is that in addition to knowledge, scientists also want proof of that knowledge. Unfortunately, proofs can be understood by everyone. As a result, it no longer affords power. In comparison, sages were much cleverer. It was easy for them to achieve the status of omniscience, what we call the 'inner sage'; unfortunately, such a title has very little to do with whether they can solve problems reliably. We know that inner sage and outer king are usually used together as a phrase. If we were to say that the reason why the inner sage has to be the smartest man in the room is for the benefit of the outer king, then we have committed the fallacy of assuming one's intentions. Fortunately, we have Zhu Xi's words to set us straight: he admits that his knowledge of all things is for the purpose of governing all under heaven.

Now, if I were to claim that Confucian ethics and moral philosophy is all wrong, I would have no evidence. I cannot even say that this body of knowledge is embarrassing. However, there is something embarrassing about this body of knowledge because certain followers have used it to usurp power. As for the inventors of this body of knowledge, by which I mean Confucius, Meng-tzu, not Zhu Xi, they are innocent. They did not acquire or enjoy any sort of power. If there are still people today attempting to revive this sort of knowledge to acquire power, we would have to use one of Meng-tzu's sayings to criticize them: 'There is nothing more shameful than being shameless.' Of course, there will be those who say,

I want to revive traditional studies to bring salvation to the people and to bolster their cultural self-esteem. In other words, they are morally superior and feel responsible for the world. All I can say to that is such a brazenly self-serving attitude is not my style; at the same time, I would fear that the clerical power is once again knocking on our door. Clerical power is clearly better than unfettered violence, that much I agree. Phoniness has always been preferable to violence. But then I think, living at the end of the twentieth century, shouldn't we hope for something a little better? Of course, one could respond to my hope by saying, isn't that too much to ask for as a Chinaman? – to which I can only cry to a wall with nothing more to say.

Overcoming the Puerile Condition

In Li Yinhe's translation of John Gagnon's *Human Sexualities,* chapter 17, 'Erotic Environment,'* describes the evolution of America's attitude toward the censorship of works containing sexual content. For this reason, it is perhaps the most interesting chapter in the whole book. In the period just before the Second World War, America's censorship of 'obscenity' was the strictest it had and has ever been. The works affected by these censorship laws extended far beyond what would be considered erotic works. As far as authors are concerned, not only were Hemingway's and Erich Maria Remarque's works banned, but even the moral thinker Leo Tolstoy's works were listed. In the second decade of this century, America's banned books included not only Joyce's *Ulysses* and D. H. Lawrence's *Women in Love*, but even *Arabian Nights*, and Remarque's *All Quiet on the Western Front* could only be published in an abridged form. As luck would have it, I happen to have a Chinese edition of *All Quiet on the Western Front*. Not only is it abridged, but the cuts

* John J. Gagnon (1931–2016) was a pioneering American sociologist in human sexuality, whose work Wang's wife, Li Yinhe, translated into Chinese.

disrupt any sense of continuity. For me, the similarities are more than intriguing. In the past, when we talked about China's hypersensitivity to books and movies, we always attributed it to the different circumstances and social policies between China and the rest of the world. However, after comparing present-day China to America in the thirties one quickly acquires a new perspective.

After the First World War, America steadily ratcheted up its censorship of erotic works. While works of a sexual nature were heavily repressed on the one hand, on the other, the amount of sexual content in serious literature surged. As a result, from the federal to the state and municipal governments emerged frighteningly long lists of banned books. The victims included far more than the abovementioned authors. Even the Bible and Shakespearean plays had to be abridged before reaching the eyes of young readers. The Bible was stripped of the 'Song of Songs.' Shakespearean works were stripped of their supposedly obscene content. The result was that young readers could not make sense of anything. Of course, it wasn't just books that were censored; movies also could not escape the gates of censorship. Movies were prohibited from showing scenes depicting prostitution, sex, nudity, drugs, mixed-race characters (!!), sexually transmitted disease, births, and anything offensive to the Christian clergy.

The strict censorship of the time was based on certain theories. One theory supposed that any open discussion about sex (which isn't critical) would lead to a proliferation of sexual activity, because sexual education is the prerequisite for sexual behavior. In other words, human sexual appetite is so strong that even the slightest provocation will force it to manifest itself. Another similar theory went like this: sex is danger, people are weak, therefore, sex must be controlled to protect people. These perspectives bear much similarity to the present attitudes toward stricter controls. In our country, there are presently people who believe that adolescent sexual misconduct has to do with books and videotapes. Some parents suggest that after reading books relating to sex, their children's grades suffered. As a result, they propose restrictions on the sexual content allowed in books and video recordings.

In my view, because these opinions were put forward by people lacking scientific training, there are inevitable points of confusion. To take the American theories from the '20s as examples, we can only say that they are scientific hypotheses. They need to be tested before they can become theories, but the worst thing is that these hypotheses are so vaguely formulated that there is no way to test them. I saw a report in a magazine with statistics showing how many adolescents charged with sexual misconduct watched 'indecent' books or pornographic videos. But this is the wrong way to arrive at a theory. The correct way to form a theory would be to point out how many of the adolescents who read 'indecent' books committed acts of sexual misconduct. If we consider the rules of probability theory, these are two entirely different probabilities. There is no fixed relationship between them and they are not mutually substitutable. As for the parents to suggest that reading books with sexual content affected their children's grades, they are in fact proposing a model of cause and effect by proposing that reading certain books will affect their children's studies. Any experienced social scientist will agree that it is difficult to determine causality. To take the parents' complaint as an example, if you want to establish causality, you must show that the kids' grades went down *because* of the books they read; you must then show that there is no cause that led to both the children's consumption of such books and their declining grades. I personally know of a factor that causes both of those effects: the child's sexual maturation. Therefore, the abovementioned parents' complaint is unfounded. Kids nowadays are well nourished and enter sexual maturity early. Their demand for information about sex comes about earlier for them than it did for their parents' generation. As far as I can tell, this is the main cause for much of the public's concern about puerile sexuality. If parents only fed their kids steamed buns and pickled mustard, that would solve the problem (by delaying the onset of sexual maturity). The above analysis shows that, regarding the question whether erotic works of art have a corruptive influence on the young, popular common sense and expert opinion arrive at two very different conclusions. Were this not the case, experts would not be considered experts.

Of course, people accuse erotic works of more than just corrupting the youth, but also corrupting society at large. On this matter, the book provides a case study, which is the Danish experiment of the '60s. In 1967, Denmark permitted erotic fiction (genuine erotica). In 1969, they permitted erotic cinema, making it legal to produce and market pornography to citizens over the age of sixteen. The experiment produced two important findings: one, Danes only bought pornography during the onset of legalization, and then they stopped or bought very little. As a result, several years after the lifting of the ban, most vendors of pornography have disappeared from Copenhagen's residential areas. At present, there are only two small neighborhoods that still traffic in the porn economy, and these small-scale economies rely primarily on tourists to survive. John Gagnon arrives at the following conclusion: 'People have many interests, of which sex is only one, and pornographic products represent only a small facet of such interest. Scarcely anyone makes sex their primary interest in life, and the number of those who make pornographic products their primary interest are fewer still.'

The second finding of the Danish experiment is that the opening up of the pornography industry had a powerful impact on criminal behaviors. The volume of pedophilia cases dropped by 80 percent. Exhibitionism decreased significantly as well. Violent crimes (rape, smut) also decreased while the rates of other crimes stayed the same. This case shows that the legalization of pornography decreases rather than increases criminal behavior. Gagnon cites the case study not to promote his own agenda, but only to share its results.

After the Second World War, America's wave of censorship began to ebb. *Human Sexualities* offers the following perspective: the decline of censorship resulted from America's evolution from a conservative, primarily rural, homogeneous Puritan population to a diverse one. The former represents an anti-immigrant, anti-Black, anti-communist, xenophobic society under the control of the so-called moral police; when America became an urbanized, industrialized society, the conditions for strict censorship no longer existed. Such an explanation has deep implications for China. Our country is also predominantly rural. As for a Puritan tradition, we don't have that history. Puritans believe that human nature is evil and needs to be controlled. Our traditional philosophy believes that humans are by nature good, but that this intrinsic goodness disappears once we grow past the 'age of innocence.' Therefore, regarding their postpubescent populations, the two cultures see eye to eye. *Human Sexualities* presents a timeline of the liberalization of America's attitude toward sex. I will list it here for reference:

Before the '40s: any nude female body part, or anything suggesting such, including raised skirts and outlines of nipples are prohibited;

1940s: backs of nude women appear in erotic magazines;

1950s: profile view of breasts;

1960s: breasts appear, vaginas appear in *Playboy* magazine

1970s: male reproductive organs appear in *Viva* and *Playgirl* magazines, female labia appear in *Penthouse* and *Playboy* magazines.

Every time a magazine went too far, the censors cried foul and warned that disaster would ensue. But in the end, there was no disaster. As a result, these people eventually met the fate of the boy who cried wolf.

Human Sexualities views the censorship of video and publishing as an example of a culturally specific sexual environment. Censorship's main target is erotic content, but serious works of art containing sexual content can also be dragged under its punishing influence. By serious works, I mean works that relate to sex without treating sex as a primary subject. These include works of great literature and film, works of sociology and anthropology, and even medical and psychological studies. On some level, serious authors and filmmakers can also be considered experts. Try thinking about censorship from their point of view. What conclusions would they draw?

In the early days of Reform and Opening-Up,* Mrs Nieh Hualing Engle and her husband Mr Paul Engle† visited China and met with a group of our nation's older authors. At their meeting, Engle asked: 'In your Chinese works, why isn't sex mentioned?' One elder

---

* This refers to the Chinese economic reforms led by Deng Xiaoping after Mao's death in 1976. Labeled as 'Socialism with Chinese characteristics' their aim was to revive the stagnant economy by moving away from collectivization and open up to private and foreign investment.

† Paul and Nieh Hualing Engle were both writers in their own right and after Paul Engle retired from directing the Iowa Writer's Workshop, they jointly created the Iowa International Writing Program, which runs to this day.

author replied: 'We in China aren't interested in that!' This was clearly pulling the foreigner's leg, as reality was not so. But the foreigner didn't take the bait, he asked: 'You in China have so many little kids, what's up with that?' The subtext to the questions is that the Chinese didn't produce all those children by pinching their noses and holding back their disgust . . . did we? Of course, we could reply: 'Yup, it was just like eating bitter medicine!' But that would have been like admitting we were a bunch of phonies. The truth is that sex is an important part of the lives of Chinese people. Our attitude toward the enjoyment of sex is no different than that of our foreign counterparts. In this area, there is really no need for a charade. Because it is important, we should naturally talk about it. Serious literature cannot avoid it; sociology and anthropology need to study it; art films should depict it. This is for the sake of science and art. But society wants to suppress the discussion, so it really isn't a question of the sexual environment but the intellectual environment.

Human Sexualities describes how the process of banning books occurred in 1920s America: a plaintiff would find a passage from a book and read it to a judge. Then he would say: would you want your kids reading *that?* Like that, Hemingway, Lawrence, and Joyce were banned. I don't know if there are any Hemingways in our country but if there are, getting published must be a headache for them. Could Hemingway write something that would satisfy the plaintiff? I think not.

I am an author myself. No author can control who

accesses their work after it is published. Suppose a serious author wrote about sex. Even if the point of their book isn't to arouse or stimulate, but to create verisimilitude, it can't be helped if a young boy finds and masturbates to his novel. It's like society wishes to dictate to the author: because these boys exist, you cannot publish literature. How unfair is that? But this isn't even the worst of it. Applying the same standard to sociologists and psychologists is even more unfair. It's as if society wants every serious writer or professional author to imagine their target reader as a sixteen-year-old boy – not even a boy with dreams and ambitions, but the kind of teenager who is fundamentally lost in life.

I am a reader myself. In my doubtless years now, I enjoy academic books and serious literature alike. But on the marketplace, there is only the seventy-two-story version of *The Decameron*, the abridged version of *The Plum in the Golden Vase*, Remarque that has been butchered into nonsense, and a bunch of books on the sociology and psychology of sex that are, frankly, complete gibberish. Recently, I bought a copy of Foucault's *The History of Sexuality*, but I can't make heads or tails of it. So now I'm looking for an English version. These politics work to my great detriment. I can say without any reservation that I am a high-level reader, but the censors treat me like a sixteen-year-old boy.

Our country's publishing industry, working according to official logic, must consider the needs of the low but not the high. A book's eligibility for publication does not depend on the existence of a readership with artistic discernment and its benefit to that group. Instead, publishing is dependent on the existence of a group without discernment and the harm a given book may cause this hypothetical reader. To me, censorship isn't a question of sexual environment but intellectual environment. Other intellectuals feel the same way. This is not a point that the book *Human Sexualities* considers. In the '20s and '30s, Americans with an intellect such as Hemingway, and others, all went to Europe. But then, Hitler showed up and kicked all the intellectuals back to America; thereby, fomenting a golden age of cultural and scientific achievements. Suppose Hitler didn't burn books and kill Jews in Europe, I dare say that compared to Europe, America would still be a backward wallow. I wouldn't go so far as to say that the scarcity of talent in our country is due only to censorship, but I can assure you, that if a Hitler showed up in America, there would be a lot more talented individuals in our nation.

If the books on the market that I want to read aren't suitable for ignorant hicks, then books suitable for developing youths aren't suitable for intellectuals either. This has nothing to do with ideology. If for example, a book like *The Diary of Lei Feng,*[*] which is good for teenagers, is translated into English, it might very well be suitable reading for the students at West Point Academy. But

---

* Lei Feng (1940–1962) was allegedly a soldier in the People's Liberation Army, portrayed as a model citizen whose example the population was encouraged to follow. His story encourages selflessness, modesty, and devotion to Mao and the Party.

for bald-headed professors, it wouldn't be very useful. Books like *Luo Lan Xiao Yu** or the novels of Qiong Yao[†] might be suitable for American high school girls (unfortunately, they already have many books of the sort), but for those intellectuals over forty with a PhD lecturing at universities in sociology departments, they wouldn't be appropriate. If you were to force them to read such books, they may gag. These types of people might read *Story of O*, even if they don't admit it when you ask them. Some might argue that since the children are our future, we should sacrifice for them. But the problem is that the price of such a sacrifice is to turn grown-ups back into kids. The result is that we are left without a future.

In Europe and America, adults and children occupy separate intellectual environments. Some books and movies cannot be seen by kids. The logic behind such a strategy is to acknowledge that adults can control themselves, and do not need courts and churches to decide who can and cannot know what. This is not simply because this material bears no harm to adults, nor is it simply because these works include knowledge that they need, but because it respects the dignity of adults. The

---

* *Luo Lan Xiao Yu* is an essay collection by Taiwanese author and broadcaster Luo Lan (1919–2015), who gained fame for narrating the life experiences of people from all walks of life.

† Qiong Yao (1938–) is the pen name of Chen Che, a hugely popular Taiwanese writer and producer whose romance novels have been adapted into more than a hundred films and TV dramas.

trend in modern society is for everyone to become an intellectual. Obstructing their access to knowledge is to obstruct their development. As Sun Longji points out in *The Deep Structure of Chinese Culture,* the Chinese people are caught in an intellectual environment characterized by the puerile condition, what Freud refers to as the anal stage. Perhaps, for various reasons, especially historical ones, we cannot avoid having some childish ways. But what then? One way is to maintain the puerile condition, the other is to overcome it, and prepare to grow up. Those who choose the former should also believe in the fictitious slogan in George Orwell's *1984* – 'ignorance is strength.' Those who choose the latter should also believe in Bacon's maxim – 'knowledge itself is power.' Of course, this next step doesn't mean rushing toward tomorrow, but it also shouldn't mean that tomorrow will never arrive.

On the Literature of Repression

There is something extraordinary about Zhang Ailing's novels, which is the depth of her understanding of the lives of women. In China, there is a type of old woman whose attitude toward young women is such that so long as the girl is not her own daughter, she wants the girl to suffer: the girl must do everything without a moment of rest, and after the work is done, the old woman will say it's not good enough; she will nag from morning to night. To use a harsh phrase – she will find fault in the wind and shadows, she will curse the mulberry tree to blame the pagoda tree. Young women nowadays wouldn't put up with this kind of life for even a day. But traditionally, all the women had to put up with it. And by the time the young bride has simmered into an old hag, she would in turn become as nasty as her old mother-in-law. Zhang Ailing has a thorough understanding of this kind of life. Her novels get to the heart of the matter. But to be perfectly honest, I don't like them. I've always felt that novels can talk about suffering and hopelessness, but they shouldn't leave the reader in a state of frustration. The reason is simple: if you weren't frustrated before reading the book, you'll be frustrated after, and if you were already frustrated, then you'd become even more frustrated. Frustration is one of the Chinese people's greatest plights. At some point, some people will simply stop feeling frustrated because they too will have become 'simmered old hags.'

In terms of tormenting others, it isn't just a women's issue but a men's issue as well; it isn't just a Chinese problem, but a world problem too. I once read a story about seafaring that touched upon the same topic. The tormentor wasn't a mother-in-law but a ship's captain. I think the story was written by Mark Twain: there was once a nasty old captain who made his sailors spend all day scrubbing the deck, wiping the windows, washing the mast. Sanitation is certainly a good thing, but scrubbing the deck twenty times a day seems a bit excessive. One day, the sailors reported that everything had been cleaned. The old man got onto the deck to inspect, only to find that there wasn't a speck of dust to be found, so he said: all right, why don't you clean the anchor then. Washing and cleaning all day left the sailors deeply frustrated, that's obvious, but there was also nothing they could do about it: surrounded by the vast ocean, even if they had wanted to quit, they would have had to wait until they reached harbor. Indeed, for a woman, living in the traditional Chinese family was just like being on a ship at sea, only that this ship will never reach harbor. If your frustration gets too much, your only choice is to jump into the sea. I'm not kidding, when it came to suicide, women in old times were experts. The conclusion to be drawn from such an analogy is this: these kinds of stories only happen in isolated settings where people are wasting their lives. These stories evoke a sense of claustrophobia.

The main point of this essay isn't to talk about Zhang Ailing or stories of seafaring, but about the mood of repression and oppression in novels. Whether it takes place in the family or on the sea, for the individual, it is about being trapped in a tiny cage; for humanity, it is an insignificant fragment of a nightmare. The bigger nightmare is the state of society, more precisely, it is one's cultural backdrop. Suppose that for a long time, society doesn't progress, lives don't improve, and no new ideas come to surface, this could be considered an intellectual's nightmare. This nightmarish state will be revealed in literature. This is precisely one of China's literary traditions. In China, people believe that nothing under heaven ever changes. When they feel frustrated in their lives, they begin to harbor a deep sense of nihilism. The best example of this literary genre is the pulp fiction of the Ming and Qing dynasties. Zhang Ailing's novels also showcase a similar mood: there is sadness but no rage; there is hopelessness but no hate; they read like something written from the deathbed. The first time I read Zhang Ailing, I was in America. I found her works rather strange. When I returned to China and read some of the works by young contemporary authors, I also had a similar feeling. Only then did I realize: maybe it was me who was strange.

The so-called literature of repression has the

following characteristic: it writes about the cage and the nightmare as if they were everything. You are either a bride living in frustration, or you are a mother-in-law annoying others; you are either blaming yourself for all your frustrations or you're being nostalgic about what you once had. In short, it's always a competition over who is more miserable. I find it hard to agree with such a world view. I majored in science. Scientists believe that there is no jail that cannot be broken out of and no nightmare that will not give way to a woken life. The only misfortune in life is one's own lack of ability. For example, for a mathematician, if you can prove Fermat's last theorem, you will win the esteem of the world's mathematical community and experience indescribable joy. The only problem is you haven't done it yet. If you are a physicist and discovered cold fusion, you would feel instant gratification. But the problem is also that you haven't done it yet. So the only takeaway is that you have to try harder. Think as if your life depended on it, that's the only way to save yourself.

It is with such an attitude that I have thrown myself into my writing career. For me, there is more to writing than talking about the same old office drama and the same old interpersonal conflicts. One could, for example, write an *Alice in Wonderland*, or a work like Italo Calvino's *Our Ancestors*. Literature could be just like science, a boundless domain in which people can launch their tsunami-like imaginations. But of course, this could also be a terrible idea. I have personally written a series of such novels about everything under the sun other than seafaring and cages. Sadly, these books are still in the hands of the editors, unable to be published. These editors even have to pose the ontological question, 'Where is this guy from? Who is he? What exactly is he writing about?'

Why I Write

Someone asked a mountaineer why he hiked – everyone knows how dangerous it is and there are no practical benefits. He answered, 'Because the mountain peak is right there.' I like this answer because it possesses a sense of humor – obviously he just wanted to hike but he had to make it seem as if it was the mountain that was making his heart itch. In addition, I like the mountaineer's pursuit, pointlessly climbing up cliffs. Hiking not only leaves you with sore muscles, but also puts you in danger of cracking your skull, which is why most people try to avoid hiking. From the perspective of thermodynamics, such a phenomenon exemplifies negative entropy. Anything that pursues disadvantage and avoids advantage is negentropic.

To say that writing is like mountaineering might sound contradictory right now. This is because in the past ten years, China has experienced a literature fever, a poetry fever, and a culture fever. Whatever the nature of the fever, the result is many people throwing themselves into writing. Some people think of me as just one of these people and caution me by saying, don't you know what year it is, why are you still writing novels (implying that we should now be having business fever, I should jump into the sea of commerce)? But my situation is different. For the first three fevers, I was studying in America, where I was not the least bit affected by the contagion. Our family creed dictates that children should not study humanities; science and technology are the only options. For that reason, the determination to write for me was exclusively a process of negative entropy. Even now, I can't understand why I do what I do, other than the fact that it is negentropic.

To say that my determination to write is a negentropic process requires further elaboration. Writing is an all-encompassing term, it does not matter what exactly one writes. Writing popular novels or romance novels should fall under the category of entropic behavior. The things I write aren't at all popular. Not only do I not make money, but sometimes I even lose some. The word *serious* in serious writers should be understood as such. As far as I can tell, most of the serious writers in this world don't truly qualify. With that said, everyone should now be able to see why what I do is truly negentropic.

The reason my parents didn't let us study humanities should be obvious. In the milieu in which I grew up, Lao She drowned himself in Taiping Lake, Hu Feng was jailed, Wang Shiwei was executed. Before that, there was Jin Shengtan's beheading and other similar examples. Of course, my old man was a pot calling the kettle black. He was a humanities professor himself but he explained that his choice had been a mistake and should not be seen as an example. The five of us brothers and sisters all ended up studying science and technology, except for my older brother. Considering my parents' foul tempers and thundering voices, you must admit that such a choice was negentropic. The exception of my older brother came about like this: in '78 when he took the college entrance exam, my older brother was the strongest miner of the Muchengjian coal mine in Beijing, his voice being even louder than my father's. In terms of beating him or yelling at him, even my father felt reluctant, so he had no choice but to let him study philosophy: he studied under the great lodestar of the logic world, Mr Shen Youding. Considering how symbolic logic is a highly specialized field (from the point of view of laymen who don't read logic papers), it really isn't very different from science and technology. From the above description, you should begin to understand my father's intentions. He wanted us each to choose a field that benefits society but is also something that ordinary people don't understand so that we could live peaceful lives. My father lived a difficult life. He loved us more than anything in the world so for him to want such an arrangement for us is only natural.

My own situation is like this: ever since I was little, I wasn't especially strong and my voice was not particularly loud, so basically, I knew my place. Even so, there was always a part of me that had the dangerous urge to write novels. When I was stationed at a commune, I met a terrible person (he was our leader, one of our country's few bad cadres), so I came up with a story about a person who, starting from his tailbone, inch by inch, became a donkey, and wrote it down to vent my heart's rage. Later, when I began to read more, I learned that Kafka had already written a similar story, which left me rather embarrassed. There was another story in which the female protagonist grew a pair of bat wings. Her hair was green, and she lived in the water. I have already burned all these works from before my twenties. To bring them up now is to explain where my dangerous urge came from. After that, I repressed my urge and after finishing my undergraduate studies, I went to study in America. After my older brother finished his master's degree, he went to study in America as well. When I was there, I started writing stories, and from then on, this dangerous urge could no longer be suppressed.

While I was in America, my father passed away. Thinking back on why he told us to study science and technology, his reasons seemed to function by an entirely different logic compared to what I had experienced in America. It reminded me of what Marshal Tukhachevsky of the Soviet Union had said to the great musician Shostakovich, 'When I was young, I was a musical prodigy. Unfortunately, my father couldn't afford to buy me a violin! If I had a violin, I would be sitting there in your orchestra pit.'* The meaning of these words is not immediately obvious, so let me explain: this

---

* Paraphrase of Marshal Tukhachevsky's words, from Shostakovich's memoir *Testimony: The Memoirs of Dmitri Shostakovich*. Harper, 1979, 97: 'How I wanted to learn the violin as a child! Father didn't buy me a violin. He never had the money. I would have been better off as a violinist.'

conversation happened in the 1930s in the Soviet Union. Not long after he said those words, the marshal breathed his last breath. In those years, they often executed marshals but not violinists. Those who jumped off buildings or hung themselves during the Cultural Revolution were predominantly the literary types. When my father was alive, he did all he could to provide us all with a violin, real or figurative: This violin could be any one of the STEM fields, and excluded only the humanities. This was completely different from what I had experienced in America, but the takeaway turned out to be the same – I should do something else; I shouldn't write novels.

As for America, everything can be summed up with the phrase: the business of America is business. This phrase implies that America is forever in the thralls of a business fever, always at a white-hot one thousand degrees. So if you had gotten the impression from what I have said so far that there was some sort of atmosphere there that encouraged writing, you would be mistaken. Even my older brother later regretted studying logic. He should have studied business administration or computer science. Even though he has yet to come up with a new logical theorem, when he sees rich people with their mansion, he can't help but complain about having shirked responsibilities toward his wife and kids.

In America, there is a powerful force pushing people toward making money. Take housing for example, some people have a small lawn, some people a few hundred acres, and others have thousands of acres. Just in terms of housing, there are infinite reasons to want to make more money. Also take cars for example, there are count-less models at a wide range of prices. If you have a lot of money, you could consider riding in the car in which Kennedy was assassinated. There are even people who buy old Soviet MiGs to fly around in. In their society, no one can stand their kids saying to their friends: my daddy is poor. If I had kids, I would be out there trying to make money as well. But writing books isn't a moneymaking profession there. If you don't believe me, just look at an American bookstore. All sorts of books crowd the shelves, as many as there are rows of toilet paper in the supermarket – if people are pouring their hearts and souls out onto rolls and rolls of toilet paper, it can't be a good business. Furthermore, there are many people whose books don't even make it onto the shelves and pile up in their homes. I don't have any kids and don't plan on having any. As a Chinese, I am a rare specimen. But every person has a face just as every tree has a bark. When other people are making money but you are off doing some suspicious work, it's hard to have much of a face.

In America, I once had a conversation with a Chin-ese American professor. He said that his daughter really showed promise. Instead of taking on a full scholarship to study anthropology at Harvard, she decided to pay her own way through an ordinary law school. To dare to go against the grain exemplifies her intellectual pedi-gree. But in fact, she only traded in a small advantage for a big advantage, accepted a small disadvantage to avoid a bigger disadvantage. If you don't believe me, just go and ask how much money lawyers make and how much anthropologists make. The professor I chatted with was a famous scholar, a man who went his own way. But when it came to his sons and daughters, he was no longer so eccentric.

After talking about America and the Soviet Union, it's time to talk about myself. At this point, I have been writing novels for eight years and published a few, but not many people have read them. Furthermore, I often receive contemptuous rejection letters. I try to stay positive and imagine: the person who wrote this letter must have gotten a scolding from his boss, so he's taking it out on me.

If you mention Wang Xiaobo, most people will think of the Sichuanese staff-wielding bandit from the Song dynasty, and not me. I am still in the process of negentropy. As an aside, human existence, civilization, and development are all negentropic processes, but here I'm talking about humanity. When it comes to me as an individual, I still can't explain what I'm doing.

As another aside, in terms of people in the process of negentropy, I am hardly the only one. In America, I met someone who set up a street side book stand selling works by Trotsky, Che Guevara, Chairman Mao, and so on. When I tried to talk to the guy, he first asked me if I was afraid of the FBI – and there are many more examples like him.

When you look at these people, you don't get a macroscopic view of water flowing downstream, apples falling to the ground, and wolves eating rabbits. Instead, what you see is water flowing up the mountain, apples flying into the air, and rabbits eating wolves. I should also add that a world with only entropy wouldn't work. Suppose everyone flowed naturally downstream, they would all end up together in the same depression, like maggots swarming in a manure pit. But this still cannot explain my behavior. It cannot be explained so long as you take the law of entropy as the preordained truth.

Of course, if I had to directly answer the question of why I write, I would say: I believe in my literary talent so I should do it. But this answer is about as believable as a murder suspect saying he didn't do it. It's up to you whether or not to believe what I say.

The Pleasure of Thinking

I

Twenty-five years ago, when I was stationed at a commune in the countryside, I brought a few books with me, one of which was Ovid's *Metamorphosis*. The people in our production team turned its pages again and again, read it over and over, until it was practically a roll of seaweed. Then, people from other production teams borrowed it, and I saw it show up in a number of other places. Each time, its shape further deteriorated. I believe that eventually, the book was read until its pages disintegrated. Even now, I can't get the image of its pathetic state out of my mind. Working in a commune meant hardship. There wasn't enough to eat. Difficulty in acclimating to a new environment led to illnesses. But the worst part was that there were no books to read. Had there been more books around, *Metamorphosis* wouldn't have met its tragic end, and we wouldn't have had to forgo the pleasure of thinking. I don't think I was alone in this experience: sitting under the eaves after dusk, watching the sky fade, feeling alone and forlorn, recognizing we were being deprived of our own lives. At the time I was still a young man, but I was already afraid that my life would go on that way, that I would grow old like that. To me, that would have been worse than death.

At the commune where I was stationed, army representatives ran our lives. Nowadays, I believe they were all good and simple people, but I also believe that in my life, no one has ever made me suffer more than they did. For them, the pleasure of thinking entailed twenty-four hours a day of Maoist thought, which meant briefings in the mornings, reports in the evening, and, for leisure, seeing musicals about how *'yagpo du'** they were. I had nothing against the songs and dances in particular, but after seeing the same show twenty times, they made me weary. Had we been caught with our books, it would have been a disaster. Even a book 'by Lu Xun' would not have been safe – the only exception was the Little Red Book. By the way, this one person did in fact get in trouble by possessing an old copy of Lu Xun. One trick that may become useful again in the future is to take an interesting book and hide it within the covers of a boring book. I didn't think I could ever derive any pleasure from religious-like rites, so I was mostly always depressed. Stories like these have been written about by other writers as well. Take Stefan Zweig, for example. He wrote a novel about this theme entitled *Chess*, which is considered a modern classic. But I don't think he fully captured our kind of suffering. The sort of suffering I'm

---

* *Yagpo du* is a Tibetan phrase meaning 'good.' It is the main theme of a popular propaganda song of the time.

talking about isn't like being locked up in a hotel with no books to read and no one to talk to, but lies in being free outside with the same sense of isolation, in the company of others who are suffering in the same way. Before us have lived countless great thinkers like Russell, Newton, Shakespeare, whose thoughts and works can free us from this suffering, but our access to their thoughts and writings had been severed. If a person wanted to find pleasure in thinking, their first wish should be for education. I admit, when faced with this sort of suffering, I lacked fortitude, but I was certainly not the worst of the lot. Take Mr Bertrand Russell, for example. When he was five years old, he felt alone and isolated; he thought: if I lived to the age of seventy, then I would be only one-fortieth of the way through my misfortune! But when he got a bit older and was exposed to thinking – to the sparks of wisdom – his ideas changed. Had he been sent to a commune, he might have killed himself.

When speaking about the pleasure of thinking, I am reminded of my father's fate. My father was a philosophy professor. In the fifties and sixties, he worked on the history of thought. In his old age, he told me that his entire academic career was like one long horror film. Every time he tried to make a point, he had to look for a niche in the great architecture of official thought, like an old hen in the crowded courtyard of a big family looking for a place to brood an egg. In the end, even though he loved his science and worked very hard, he was never able to find pleasure from a life of thinking, only horror. After a lifetime of research, he only left behind some ruins and vestiges that were anthologized in a book called *Logical Investigations*, published posthumously. As everyone knows, for a scholar of his generation to leave behind even only one book was not bad at all. This was precisely because in those years, there were people who wanted to make the Chinese mind completely insipid. In our country, there are only very few people who feel there is pleasure in thinking, but there are quite a few people who have felt the horror of even trying to think. This is why even now, many people believe that this is how thinking should taste.

2

After the Cultural Revolution, I read a piece of nonfiction by Mr Xu Chi about Goldbach's conjecture. It was a rather romantic essay. When someone writes about things they don't really understand, it is easy to romanticize. In my opinion, for a scholar to be able to exchange ideas with peers is a basic pleasure. When Mr Chen Jingrun* was sitting in a tiny room by himself proving mathematical theorems, he would have been in desperate need of foreign periodicals to read, and of the

---

* Mr Chen Jingrun (1933–1966) was a Chinese mathematician who made significant contributions to analytic number theory. At the end of the Cultural Revolution, Mr. Xu Chi wrote a biography about him which became a national sensation.

opportunity to converse with foreign colleagues, but he couldn't. So perhaps he could be considered unfortunate. Of course, he was probably more fortunate than people with no theorems to prove at all. To spend ten years proving a theorem, even if the moment of success feels like absolute bliss, doesn't add up to much average happiness. But to sit fruitlessly alone is so much worse. Had I known about mathematical theories when I was at the commune, I would have done as Mr Chen did; even if I would not have been able to prove anything in the end, I wouldn't have had any regrets; a story like that would have been even more tragic than the story Mr Xu had written. On the other hand, my highest sympathy isn't reserved for those who were deprived of the pleasures of learning, exchanging, and advancing ideas. I reserve my highest sympathies for those who have been deprived of *interestingness* altogether.

After the Cultural Revolution, I read a short story by Mr Ah Cheng about playing chess as an intellectual youth. It was also a very romantic story. Of all the chess games I've played in life, four-fifths of them took place during my time at *the* commune. There, I went from a not-too-bad chess player to a hopelessly mediocre hand. Whenever I think about the words 'chess' and 'commune' together, my body revolts. To play chess only because there was nothing else to do is tantamount to jerking off. I would never put something so boring into a story.

It is to the person who eats the same food everyday, does the same work every day, watches the same eight model operas* so many times that they know the next half of every line, that I offer my highest sympathy. Here I echo a line by Bertrand Russell, 'To know the long and short, thick and thin, is the basis of happiness.' Indeed, most of what is diverse is created by subtle thinkers. Of course, some will disagree. To them, uniformity is the basis of happiness. Lao-tzu wanted everyone to 'empty their mind and fill their bellies.' I don't like the sound of that at all; Confucians of the Han dynasty eliminated the Hundred Schools and ordained Confucianism as the sole discipline. To me that was a vile thing to do. Sir Thomas More imagined utopia in the finest detail but, like Mr Russell, I would not want to live under such circumstances. At the end of the line are those good and simple army representatives. They wanted to wipe everything out of my mind except for that 270-page *Little Red Book*. In some domains of life, a certain degree of monotony and mechanical repetition is unavoidable, but thinking should not be included in such domains. A wandering mind isn't necessarily exceptional, but what is exceptional is logical and novel thinking. The greatest

* During China's Cultural Revolution (1966–1976), Jiang Qing, the wife of Chairman Mao Zedong, produced revolutionary model operas. They were the only officially permitted literary form at the time and told stories of revolutionary struggles and ideals. Many were made into movies. The operas were considered revolutionary and modern, in contrast to the traditional Peking operas, which were mostly regarded as 'bourgeois' and therefore banned.

misfortune in this world that we live in is that some people categorically reject novelty.

I think the happiest period of my life was when I first started college because to me science was a novelty. Its logic was complete and flawless, something rare in this mundane world. At the same time, it revealed the intellectual might of our forebears. It felt like a contest against a brilliant chess player – though outmatched at every turn, at least I was able to marvel at their moves. Among my classmates and people my age, many had the same experience. Despite repetitive actions like eating, defecating, and fornicating also offering some pleasures, these were much too simple to even compare to this other kind of pleasure. Art can also offer similar kinds of pleasure, but only at the hands of truly great masters at the level of Newton, Leibniz, or Einstein. For now, no Chinese artist rises quite to that level. But to be frank, the only works that can offer the pleasure of thinking are the ones that epitomize human wisdom. Anything less can only bring misery; and these medi-ocre creations tend to be motivated by utility.

3

The idea that there is a need to 'indoctrinate' the organ of human thinking (the brain) is still very much alive today. I believe that the mind is the human organ crucial to perceiving supreme happiness, even more so than the organs of perception. Shoving 'useful' thoughts into it seems suspicious at best. Some people say that the brain is a tool for competition, so one should learn to speak before birth and memorize Tang poetry before the age of three. But if this is the way you use it, how could you ever find joy? Truly troubling. Sure, knowledge can bring happiness, but if you distill it into a pill and swallow it, it no longer bears any pleasure. Of course, if anyone wants to treat their children like that, it is none of my business. I can only express sympathy for those children. Still others believe that the brain is a tool to make themselves look virtuous. To that end, they study a bunch of aphorisms and principles – in reality, they are only trying to make themselves seem better than they are. Truly pretentious. It pains me just to think about it, and I condone it. The worst are those people who use all sorts of reasons to eviscerate the diversity of thoughts necessary for happiness. They mainly reason it has to be done in the name of morality, but the standards they use are dubious. They believe that if you could fill the brains with good thoughts, there would be peace under heaven. To this end, they are willing to treat young people the way the army representatives treated me back in the day. But if thinking is the most important facet of human life, then changing other people's thoughts under a utilitarian banner is basically like murdering them for their happiness. It just does not make sense.

Some people believe that a person should be filled with only high-minded thoughts and be relieved of all the lowly ones. Such an idea may sound good, but it fills me with terror because I am precisely an amalgam of high and low thoughts; if a part of that is removed, my identity becomes a question. I hold all the respect in the world for high-minded gentlemen, but if you had to pluck out my brain and replace it with theirs, I would refuse, unless you could somehow prove to me that I am evil to the extreme and deserve death. So long as a person is alive, the continuity of their thoughts ought to be guaranteed. Not to mention, the high and the low are all being measured from one's own perspective. If I accepted them unconditionally, it would be like letting well-thinking hens lay eggs in my brain. But I would never concede that the thing on my neck is actually a chicken nest. Back in the day, the army representatives saw me as a lowly person. They wanted to force their thoughts and lifestyle onto me, like a brain transplant. Henry Fielding once said that there are few, if any, people who are both good and great. Therefore, this sort of brain transplant would have given me not only goodness but also stupidity. I hate to say it in such a utilitarian way, but in the real world, stupid people can't accomplish anything. Of course I hope to become a better person, but only my betterment is the result of having become smarter, and not the other way around. Besides, Heraclitus explained long ago that good and evil are one. Just like uphill and downhill are the same road. If you don't know what is evil, how can you know what is good? So the thing they really want is for people to have no thoughts of their own at all.

Suppose I believed in God (which I don't), and was troubled over the question of good and evil: I would beg God to make me smart enough to be able to distinguish between the two. I would never ask Him to make me stupid enough to allow others to inculcate me with their standards. If God asked me to take up the responsibility of inculcating others, I would beseech Him to make me choose between that task and Hell, and I would unhesitatingly choose the latter.

4

Were I to cite the kindest moment in my life, I would cite the beginning of my time as an intellectual youth. Back then, I thought only about the liberation of mankind and not at all about myself. Still, I must admit that at that time I was truly stupid. Not only didn't I accomplish anything, but I contracted a disease, and after tossing my helmet and abandoning my armor, I fled back to the city. It is now my belief that stupidity is the worst sort of misery; diminishing the intellectual capacity of mankind is the worst sort of atrocity. To teach ignorance is the worst crime committed by otherwise good people. Therefore, we should never lower our guard against good people. Had I been duped by an evil scheming villain, I could come to terms with it; but to have been duped by kind, dimwitted people is intolerable.

Were I to cite the least kind moment in my life, I would cite the present. Perhaps this is because I received some education, or perhaps because I have grown older, but if you were to ask me to go liberate a group of people, I would first want to ask who these people are and why they need help; then I would ask whether helping them is within my abilities; finally, I would wonder whether it actually helps anyone for me to run off to Yunnan to dig holes. When I think about it this way, I definitely wouldn't want to join a commune. If the authorities forced me to go, I would still have to go, but all the holes we would dig into the verdant mountains and all the landslides we would cause wouldn't be my fault. Normally, people believe that kind but stupid people are innocent. If this stupidity were caused by nature, then I would agree. But people are able to cultivate their intelligence, so stupidity later in life is no longer innocent – besides, there's nothing more convenient than playing the fool. Of course, that isn't to say the army representatives back in the day were crooks pretending to be dumb – I still believe they were good people. My conclusion is: assuming good and evil are relative, these moral judgments must be made with a fully developed intellect and expansive knowledge. Yet, when you actually try to convince someone who thinks they can tell good from evil that they should first develop their intellect and expand their knowledge, they will always say that you are asking them to take the long road. Not only would they refuse, but they would harbor resentments. I wouldn't want to offend anyone over anything too trivial.

Of course, I now have my own standards of good and evil and I don't seem to behave any worse than anyone else. To me, stupidity, paranoia, and intellectual bankruptcy are the greatest evils. By this standard, whenever someone says I am good, that's when I am at my most evil; whenever someone says I am evil, that's when I am at my best. Of course, I wouldn't want to push this standard onto other people because I believe that smart, open-minded, knowledgeable, unique people are the most trustworthy. With regard to this concept, I believe after the period of 'eliminate the Hundred Schools of Thought,* ordain Confucianism alone,' our country has missed out on a lot of opportunities.

Our people have always been locking up knowledge and repressing thoughts to inculcate goodness. As a result, many thoughtful individuals missed their opportunities to learn, exchange, and advance ideas, and died before discovering the pleasure of thinking. The thought that my father was one such case leaves me with a heavy heart; and when I think about the fact that the number of such thoughtful individuals are as countless as the sand in the River Ganges, I slip toward despair. The source of all this tragedy are of course various real-world problems. Great figures tend to think that if everyone in the world were as good as they were – or more precisely, thought the way they thought: 'think no evil' and 'battle the wolf of selfishness,' then the world could be saved. The people who propose these ideas thought no evil and weren't selfish to begin with, but of course they wouldn't know what evil thoughts and

---

* The Hundred Schools of Thought were philosophical currents and schools of thought that flourished between 600 and 221 BCE. The intellectual society of this era consisted of itinerant scholars, who often served as advisers to state rulers on methods of government, war, and diplomacy.

selfishness were. That's why they are basically saying: what I don't have, you shouldn't have either. Countless thinkers were smothered because of that. The countless thoughtful individuals, as numerous as the granules of sand in the River Ganges, amount to a massive resource. Trying to contain their thoughts is like trying to stuff the ocean into a bottle. Truthfully, I see it still happening, that is to say, the search for stupid solutions to the world's problems. On these grounds, I believe that since the Han dynasty, our country has been committing an ongoing intellectual massacre; and the fact that I can think this means that I am one of the few lucky survivors. Aside from expressing my sorrow for the current situation, I can't think of much else.

5

Even though I have reached my doubtless years,* there is still one thing that confuses me: how come there are so many people who hate new and interesting things? The ancients have a saying: had heaven not produced Confucius, the eons would have remained like night. But I believe just the opposite. Suppose that somewhere in history there was a great sage who suddenly discovered all novelties and things interesting, revealing the ultimate truth such that there would be nothing left to be discovered, then I would prefer to be born in a time before such a great sage existed. The reason is that if

---

* Idiomatic expression meaning 'middle aged.'

the ultimate truth has already been discovered, then the only thing left for humanity to do would be to judge everything based on this truth. Ever since the Han dynasty, this is how the Chinese people have lived. I am not at all interested in such a life.

I believe that, of all the intellectual activities a person can undertake, nothing is simpler than placing a value judgment. Even if you were a male bunny, you would already make value judgments – big gray wolf bad, female bunny good. But the bunny doesn't know his nine-by-nine multiplication table. This fact explains why people with no other real abilities so love the domain of values. To place a value judgment upon oneself at least requires some sacrifice; to judge others is simply too easy, too comfortable. To say something this crass leaves me feeling a bit ashamed, but I offer no apologies. It is because unsophisticated people have caused us far too much misery.

Of all the value judgments, the worst is the following: you think too much, too deeply, beyond what most people can understand, and that's wrong. When we are experiencing the pleasure of thinking, we aren't hurting anyone; the sad thing is that intellectualism always causes some people to feel left out. Of course, the pleasure of a thought cannot be felt by everyone, but that is not our responsibility. I see no reason to eliminate these kinds of pleasures, unless you count cruel envy as one of the reasons – in this world there are people who enjoy nuance and people who enjoy purity; I've never come across someone who enjoyed nuance to envy or harm those who enjoyed purity, but I have seen plenty of the opposite. If I can be said to know a thing or two about the arts and sciences, it is because they flow from the mighty river of the pleasure of thinking. The river is there for the benefit of all people, and not as some would have it, flowing for a few alone. In the same way, the people who take pleasure in thinking weren't born for those few either.

For an intellectual, the desire to become a champion of thinking is more important than the desire to become a champion of morality. Certainly, people are free to not think and be stupid; on this point, I have no disagreement. But the problem lies in whether people should have the right to think and make themselves smarter. The people who appreciate the former freedom think that overly complicated thoughts will give people headaches. That seems reasonable enough. But if you take a farmer from deep in the mountains and asked him to work in a chemical factory in the city, he too will get a headache from all the complicated plumbing. That's not a reason to eliminate chemical engineering. Therefore, it is good if simple people can see what they cannot understand as something that does not concern them.

If I were to once again find that the world around me is filled with Cultural Revolution era army representatives and moralizers, I would be surprised, but I would no longer be afraid. This is because I have already lived to the age of forty-two. At university, I once met a professor who spreads mathematics like it was happiness itself. He has made learning math a joy. I have met people who have inspired my search for wisdom. I have also been fortunate enough to have read books that I wanted to read – it has been an eclectic selection from Bertrand Russell's *A History of Western Philosophy* to Victorian era underground novels. The latter selection was extremely profane, but in the end I got to read the naughty ones too. Of course, I am most grateful to those who wrote the best books – for example, George Bernard Shaw, Mark Twain, Italo Calvino, Marguerite Duras, and so on, but I hold no grudge against those who wrote bad books either. I myself have written a few books. Though they haven't yet become available to mainland readers, at least I've finally felt something of the joy of creation. These tiny pleasures make me feel like I have done something with my life, which makes me happier than my father ever was, and happier than the young people who are currently suffocating in an intellectual vacuum. As someone who has experienced both happiness and misery, I wish for the next generation to have more space to experience happiness, more space than what I was afforded. And of course, this call is aimed at those whose ambition it is to become teachers of morality, like the army representatives back in the day.

Using Golden Age *to Talk About the Art of Fiction*

The book *Golden Age* includes five medium-length stories.* Of these, the story entitled 'Golden Age' was begun when I was twenty years old and was not completed until I was nearly forty. Within that time, it went through many revisions. When reading my old drafts now, just about every sentence leaves me in a cold sweat. Only the last draft doesn't have that effect. In this thirty-thousand-character story, there are obviously still imperfections, but I no longer feel the urge to edit them out. This shows that it's possible to write a story in this way. Even though it's difficult, it's not impossible. This kind of writing is an author's pursuit of perfection. I believe that each author has a particular sense of perfection, but that this perfection cannot be pursued every time. It was said that Friedrich Dürrenmatt also wrote *The Judge and His Hangman* over many years. Upon its completion, he said: I can never write a novel like this again. This means he also wrote like that. A person

---

* In 2022, Astra House published an edition of *Golden Age* that contained three of the stories – 'Golden Age'; 'At Thirty, A Man'; and 'Years as Water Flow.'

cannot make every piece of work perfect, but of course, perfection would be best.

Once, a girl asked me how to write a story, adding that she was thinking about writing something. I explained to her my process of writing *Golden Age*. The next time I saw her, I asked how her writing was coming along. She said, after hearing about how hard it was to write, she gave up on the idea. Actually, in this book, most of the chapters didn't have to go through such an arduous process of revision. But I do encourage all writers to give it a try. It's good for you.

Many parts of the book touch upon sex. This kind of writing can lend itself to controversy, inviting accusations of bawdiness. I don't know why the writing came out like that. Thinking back on it, it wasn't written for the sake of controversy or bawdiness but as the reflection of an age. As we all know, the sixties and seventies in China were an asexual age. Only in an asexual age does sex become an interesting topic. It's just like how during famines, eating becomes an important topic. The ancients have a saying: hunger and lust are natural. Wanting to love and to eat is an essential part of human nature. Their deprivation becomes an obstacle to human existence.

Of course, these obstacles are not the main themes of my story. The main theme is still a reflection on the human condition. The pivotal logic is that our lives are so full of obstacles – how damned interesting! This kind of logic is called black humor. I think black humor is my aura, I was born with it. The characters in my stories are always laughing, never crying. I think it's more interesting this way. The people who like my stories often talk about how they laughed from beginning to end and found them very interesting, etcetera. This shows that my works have their own readership. Of course, some authors believe that crying is more moving. The characters under their pens never laugh, only cry. That's also a way to write. They also have their own readership. A friend once said that none of my stories have ever moved her. She's the crying type. She read my story by mistake and felt disappointed. I want to explain this because I don't want anyone else to read my stories by mistake and feel disappointed.

Readers of serious literature are fewer and fewer, but their aptitude has greatly increased. In modern society, literature has become like opera, a form of high art. Literature has lost a portion of its readers – for example, those looking for moral guidance, those looking for political intrigue, those feeling sexually frustrated, those looking for some thrill, those with nothing to do and time to kill; only those who are interested in reading serious fiction are left. Literature has also lost many of its authors – some have jumped into the sea of commerce, others have turned to writing TV and movie scripts, the only ones left are those interested in writing serious fiction. I think this is a good thing.